FIC   Khuri, Ilyas.

           The journey of little
           Gandhi.

$17.95

DATE			

APR   1996

BAKER & TAYLOR

THE JOURNEY OF LITTLE GANDHI

EMERGENT LITERATURES

Emergent Literatures is a series of international scope that makes available, in English, works of fiction that have been ignored or excluded because of their difference from established models of literature.

THE JOURNEY OF LITTLE GANDHI

Elias Khoury

Foreword by Sabah Ghandour
Translated by Paula Haydar

University of Minnesota Press
Minneapolis
London

Originally published as *Rihlat Ghandi al-saghir* © 1989 by Dār al-Ādāb, Beirut

Published by the University of Minnesota Press
2037 University Avenue Southeast, Minneapolis, MN 55455-3092
Printed in the United States of America on acid-free paper

Library of Congress Cataloging-in-Publication Data

Khūrī, Ilyās.
    [Riḥlat Ghāndī al-ṣaghīr. English]
    The journey of little Gandhi / Elias Khoury ; translated by Paula Haydar.
      p. cm. — (Emergent literatures ; 15)
    ISBN 0-8166-1995-6
    I. Title. II. Series.
PJ7842.H823R5413   1993
892'736—dc20   93-4743
                                       CIP

For both of you, Abla and Talal

For Adnan, who gave me the gift of Arabic

Paula

*A face is only one, yet when it's seen
in many mirrors, multiplies itself.*

Ibn Arabi

Foreword

Sabah Ghandour

Hayden White differentiates between two types of discourse. The first is a discourse that narrates: "It adopts openly a perspective on the world and reports it." The second is a discourse that narrativizes: "It feigns to make the world speak itself ... as a story."[1] Elias Khoury's *The Journey of Little Gandhi* "feigns" to make its fictional world speak for itself; it narrates itself as a "story." By situating himself inside his narrative, the narrator-author accomplishes two goals: first, to dismiss the idea of the godlike author who knows everything; second, to invite us, the readers, to participate in the act of reading/writing, in the discovery of Gandhi's and other embedded "journeys." *The Journey of Little Gandhi* could be characterized as an "open text" as defined by Kamal Abu Deeb: "It is an unmolded text. By its refusal to be molded, the text rejects becoming a rite for authority's practice."[2] More than any of Khoury's other works, this novel explicitly draws our attention to the act of narrating and to that of writing.[3] Little Gandhi's "journey" is a metaphor for writing, exploration, and discovery.

   The Journey of Little Gandhi differs from other novels written on the Lebanese civil war by its method of narration. This departure from the traditional narrative mode leads to a change in the narrative structure of the novel.[4] *Little Gandhi* consists of seven chapters of various lengths. The first chapter is five pages long; the second chapter is slightly more than double that at eleven pages; the third chapter is twenty-four pages long; and so on.[5] Then the chapters begin to shrink till we reach the last one, which is only two pages long. This structure is inextricably intertwined with the contents of the novel. The beginning and ending of the novel telling of the death of Little Gandhi require not an enormous space but rather an abridged one. The "journey" of Little Gandhi, which constitutes the bulk of the narrative, from his birth in Mashta Hasan to his death during the Israeli invasion of Lebanon in 1982, requires a more substantive space to contain the various incidents and events. As we plunge deeper in the narrative, we encounter numerous stories and surprises as if we were opening a Pandora's box or a Russian nesting doll.

We read on the first page of the novel, "I'm telling the story and it hasn't even ended yet. And the story is nothing but names. When I found out their names, I found out the story." Are the many stories narrated in *Little Gandhi* connected by proper nouns? We move from one story to another, from one incident to another by merely mentioning names and associations. The narrator-author asks and investigates but he keeps "finding holes in the story." In the narrator's attempt to relate Little Gandhi's journey, we also find out that the real story is that of life and death because the story is "about those who couldn't escape" from the atrocities of the civil war and the Israeli invasion. It is the story of Gandhi, Alice, the narrator, and many others who are obliged to live in the midst of war; they either survive or perish. So we have an equation: the story equals life with all its beautiful and horrifying surprises, with its expected and unexpected events, with its sweetness and bitterness.

Are we then reading stories similar in their form and the delineation of incidents to the stories told by Sheherazade to King Shariar in *A Thousand and One Nights*? What is the frame-story the novel presents? Does this comparison between *A Thousand and One Nights* and *Little Gandhi* end with the structure of the novel or does it go beyond that? Sheherazade tells stories to save herself from death and to give the tyrant another chance to reconsider his verdict. Who buys life in *Little Gandhi* when we know that most of the characters in this novel die or disappear? Does life within this context equal writing and creativity? Why has Elias Khoury chosen this narrative structure for his novel?

The first principal frame for this novel is the Lebanese civil war and the invasion of Lebanon by Israel, specifically its invasion of Beirut. This war atmosphere presents the main backdrop of this novel, for it grants or denies the characters life and death. Little Gandhi was killed when the Israelis reached Beirut on September 15, 1982. Alice, the prostitute, disappeared during the 1984 events in Beirut.[6] The development of these historical events is contained within this frame. Invasion in this context equals death, and writing after the nightmare of invasion provides life and re-creates the memory of individuals and groups. The second frame, which is equally important, represents the narrator-author as a character in the novel. This frame intertwines with the third frame represented by Alice, who tells the stories to the narrator till she disappears during the events of 1984.

Many incidents spring from or converge in the last two frames. The narrator looks for Alice so that she can tell him about Little Gandhi's "journeys," for Little Gandhi met Alice by chance and had told her his stories. And through Little Gandhi via Alice we know the story of his son Husn, his work as a hairdresser and his relationships with women, and many other stories. Thus we move from one story to another, from one incident to another, as if they have no logical or chronological connection except for being connected by names. This distinction in narration, which resembles that of *A Thousand and One Nights,* captures the daily lived experiences manifested by the languages of the characters. The different languages employed in the novel go beyond the classical distinction between modern standard and colloquial Arabic. The many-leveled languages—the written memory, the forgotten memory, the church, the orientalist, the macho, and other languages, which go along with the "tricks" of narration—give us one of the avenues for reading the text.[7]

The language of a novel is the system of its "languages," as Bakhtin observes.[8] In *Little Gandhi,* we do not find a language that tells mere facts as do the ones we get in traditional novels. Even when the narrator reports a certain incident, his language is filled with questionings and ambiguities: "I met Abd al-Karim by coincidence, but her, I don't know how I met her. Abd al-Karim, nicknamed Little Gandhi, was a shoe shiner. He never shined my shoes, but everyone had told me about him. I ran into him once and we talked for a long time. But her, I don't know, maybe another coincidence." In the new novel, as Sabry Hafez puts it, "Language has abandoned its declamatory phrases."[9] Moreover, *Little Gandhi* does not employ the various languages randomly; each language has its own function, which is related to the social status of the speaker and the related topic. What is important about these languages is their being "dialogical," and within this dialogue we can determine the nexus, the relation between these languages and the lived experiences. We have, for example, the story of Mr. Davis, the American philosophy professor at the American University of Beirut, and his dog, which was struck and killed by a car. After the car's driver spat on the dog saying, "It's only a dog," Mr. Davis felt that "the East is barbaric. If not for India and the real Gandhi, the East would've remained barbaric." Mr. Davis had lived for a long time in Lebanon and tried to speak Arabic with a Beiruti accent. He loved the East, its "spices," and the Arabs, but he was not able to understand the behavior of the car driver, nor could he comprehend the "other's" point of view. This failure to understand the "other" in the midst of this "other" immediate environment drove Mr. Davis to use stereotypical phrases about the East, instead of questioning the failure of his project in this East that he had "oriented," as Edward Said says. The East became to him anecdotes about spices and the Arabs. This incident implicates the generalized language about the Arabs and demonstrates the failure of those who adopt such a language.

The dialogue that took place between Little Gandhi and the Reverend Amin is another example that proves language is not transparent; it is unable to convey the intended meaning:

> "Blessed are the meek, for they shall inherit the earth."
> 'What do you mean by blessed, Reverend?"
> Gandhi asked.
> "Blessed means how lucky they are. How lucky you are, Gandhi, because you saw the green horse. No one but John the Baptist has ever seen that horse."

"Send my best to John the Baptist, Your
Highness."

Little Gandhi's answer demonstrates his inability to understand the Reverend Amin's rhetorical language. Despite the
Reverend's attempt to use standard modern Arabic and the
colloquial in this dialogue, he was not able to explain to
Gandhi the religious beliefs in a simplified accessible vo-
cabulary. Language, instead of being a means of commu-
nication and understanding, becomes an obstacle and a
hindrance for its intended purpose. Here discourse does
not reflect a certain situation, for it is in itself a situation.[10]
Whereas Mr. Davis understands the world from a cultural
angle, the Reverend Amin understands it from a religious
and class perspective. The Reverend, who believes that
"America [is] the model of this new world that Christ had
saved," hates the simple life the Americans advocate. Little
Gandhi feels that he cannot understand his own language,
especially when the young bearded American youth, who
"discovered the simple life through Gandhi," speaks Arabic:

> *"God grant you a long life, Reverend. You all*
> *speak English. I don't understand a word. What's-*
> *his-name starts speaking Arabic like he's speaking*
> *English. I don't understand a word. I . . ."*

While Gandhi feels alienated from his language, Rima, his
son's girlfriend, does not. She speaks as if "putting spaces
between her words." Rima uses three languages each day.
She speaks German with her German mother, French at
work, and Arabic with her friends. Rima does not question
her use of these three languages. Put differently, these languages do not lead Rima to be aware of her situation. For

her character or her identity is constituted among these languages, and thus her subjectivity challenges the unitary understanding of the term. In fact, Rima's subjectivity shows that the distinction between the language expressing that subjectivity and the lived situation is indeed blurred and unclear. Does the text tell us that the identity is disintegrating or incomplete because Beirut, the city in which all the characters lived, is the one that travels from "the Switzerland of the East to Hong Kong, to Saigon, to Calcutta, to Sri Lanka[?] It's as if we circled the world in ten or twenty years. We stayed where we were and the world circled around us." Beirut is not only a place where the novel's events take place; Beirut is, in fact, the major character in the novel—its importance supersedes that of Little Gandhi. As Kamal Abu Deeb notes, "Life itself is the heroine. The place and the people whom Elias Khoury lies to us about are the heroes because they survive."[11] Moreover, the movement of Beirut from Switzerland to Sri Lanka is a parodic confusing of metropolis and national space, as well as that of the colony, that reveals all three to be figures of designation: they mark difference in time and not in geography.

Like the many-leveled languages we encounter in *Little Gandhi,* temporality is also fragmented into many times. The temporality of this novel is not chronological; it does not have a clear beginning and end. Rather, it points to "a time that does not acknowledge the historical traditional sequence"[12] of events, for the past is constantly diffused into the present, and the present invariably reaches out for the past to interrogate it. One of the historical periods that this text problematizes is the one preceding the war going back to the beginning of this century: "The Turks left and then came the French, and under the French everything changed. The Jesuits took over everything and we no longer knew in which country we were living. One minute the State of Beirut, the next Greater Lebanon, the next I don't know what." The second of these temporalities refers to the time of war itself and its development into many "Lebanese wars." While these different temporalities highlight the various ideological, political, and social issues, they also function as connectors and references to the various embedded stories.

The function of the embedded stories, as Todorov notes, is to allow the main story to reach its maximum development so that we can move to another event where a character becomes "a potential story that is the story of his life. Every new character signifies a new plot. We are in the realm of narrative-men."[13] The embedded stories in *Little Gandhi* could stand as stories by themselves, and they mainly refer to life, death, birth, or destruction. We read the stories of the many names enumerated in the first page of the novel, and we move from one story to another by associations and the mentioning of names. Most of the stories in *Little Gandhi* originate in names, and they revolve around death and writing: "If Kamal al-Askary hadn't died, then Alice wouldn't have met up with Gandhi, and if she hadn't met Gandhi, then he wouldn't have told her his story. And if Gandhi hadn't died, Alice wouldn't have told me the story. And if Alice hadn't disappeared, or died, then I wouldn't be writing what I am writing now." Death allows the narrator to tell everything. Put differently, death allows him to mix the real with the imaginary, for "he has borrowed his authority from death. In other words, it is natural history to which his stories refer back."[14] The narrator-author who is "narrating and writing" discovers that he is "digging in a deep well," for writing, as I have indicated elsewhere,[15] is a discovery into the known and the unknown. Elias Khoury does not offer any definitive answers for the dilemmas of life, war, and invasion. The novel's structure with its embedded stories parallels the "Lebanese war" with its seemingly unresolved events. Although the "journey" is tragic for most of the characters in this novel, the narrator, like Sheherazade, wards off death by his stories. Writing in this context provides life and continuation to the act of creativity in the midst of war and destruction. Moreover, writing becomes a game of names and naming as *Little Gandhi* tells us. When Abd Karim Husn al-Ahmadi al-Mughayiri was nicknamed Gandhi by an American professor, he resented the name at first. Then when the Reverend Amin added "Little," he accepted it, although he preferred to be called Abu Husn.[16] To give something or someone a name is to give that entity or person an identity. But then a serious question arises: who possesses the power to name things or individuals? to construct their identities?

Notes

1. Hayden White, "The Value of Narrativity in the Representation of Reality," *Critical Inquiry* 7 (Autumn 1980), 7.

2. Kamal Abu Deeb, "Al-hadatha, al-sulta, al-nass," *Fusul* 4 (1984), 46.

3. This issue is examined in my article on *Gandhi* in *Mawakif* 72 (Summer 1993).

4. See my foreword to Elias Khoury's *Gates of the City* (Minneapolis: University of Minnesota Press, 1993), xv-xvi.

5. The reference here is to the Arabic text, which the English translation generally matches.

6. The opposition forces reclaimed West Beirut, pushing out the forces loyal to President Amin al-Jumayyil.

7. Muhammad Barrada, "Al-Ta`dud al-Lughawi fi al-Riwaya al-`Arabiyya," *Mawakif* 69 (Autumn 1992), 173.

8. M. M. Bakhtin, *The Dialogic Imagination* (Austin: University of Texas Press, 1983), 262.

9. Sabry Hafez, "Al-Riwaya wal-Waqi`," *Al-Naqid* 26 (August 1990), 39.

10. Michael Holquist, *Dialogism: Bakhtin and His World* (New York and London: Routledge, 1990), 63.

11. Kamal Abu Deeb, "Al-nass wal-haqiqah,"*Mawakif* 69 (Autumn 1992), 158.

12. Hafez, "Al-Riwaya wal-Wagi`," 37.

13. Tzvetan Todorov, *The Poetics of Prose* (Ithaca, N.Y.: Cornell University Press, 1984), 70.

14. Walter Benjamin, *Illuminations,* edited and with an intro. by Hannah Arendt (New York: Schocken Books, 1976), 94.

15. See my foreword to *Gates of the City.*

16. In most of the Arab countries, the fathers are usually called by the names of their eldest sons; Abu Husn means "the father of Husn."

1

But they're talking.

I see their images in front of me, fading away behind their eyes. Eyes that vanish, and water. Lots of water, covering everything. And distant voices; voices that seem to be distant. I summon the images before me and listen.

I don't know who's talking or who's listening. I'm talking. I'm the one who's been talking all along. But I'm not sure. Is it my voice or the images? Why are they like that? I see their images while they themselves dissipate like water. Water doesn't dissipate, water just takes you and goes. They're in the water, and they're all just like the water. I'm telling the story and it hasn't even ended yet. And the story is nothing but names. When I found out their names, I found out the story. Abd al-Karim, Alice, Suad, the Reverend Amin, the American Davis, the dog, the barber, Spiro with the hat, Salim Abu Ayoun, Doctor Atef, Doctor Naseeb, Abu Jamil the impresario, Lieutenant Tannous al-Zaim, the second dog, Madame Nuha Aoun, Husn, Ralph, Ghassan, Lillian Sabbagha, Constantine Mikhbat, Abu Saeed al-Munla, "The Leader," Fawziyya, Husn the son of Abd al-Karim, Abd al-Karim the son of Husn, the Assyrian Habib Malku, the Aitany boy, and al-

Askary, et cetera, et cetera, and the White Russian woman, et cetera, every one of them died. They went to this et cetera thing and didn't come back. I don't know if Najat died, but the old baker Rashid died for sure. And the rest, I don't know. Even the death of Abd al-Karim, who opens the whole story, is uncertain. I didn't see him die. Actually, I wasn't even there when he died, and when I went to visit him at his house, I didn't find any trace of him. Not of him, or his wife, or his daughter, or the barber. And I didn't search for them. I met Alice in a cheap hotel called the Salonica. The first time I went to it, I thought the owner was a Greek from Mount Athos, where lots of monks live, but it turned out to be just some small hotel, situated next to the Starco building, which had been demolished by bombs. It was full of retired prostitutes, barmaids, whores, and some soldiers. Alice was a maid in the hotel. She told me she was a maid, but I don't know, and I don't know why she told me all those stories. When I lost track of Alice, and the hotel disappeared in 1984, I remembered Abd al-Karim and decided to write these stories down. I discovered that the things Alice told me weren't lies. A woman in love doesn't lie. Alice wasn't in love and she didn't lie. That's how she was, told lies like everyone else, but she told me everything, and all of it was true.

Alice vanished, and they began dying right before my eyes. Was it I who was killing them, or am I simply a narrator telling their stories?

I walk, and Abd al-Karim's shadow walks beside me. I see his small frame and broken teeth and thick, tawny neck. I see everything, and when I ask him about Alice, I discover he's merely a shadow. Abd al-Karim has become a shadow that fills my eyes. When he died, no one knew about it. He died when death ceased to have any value.

"Death has always been cheap," Alice said when she was telling me his story. But she was lying, because she knew death does have a price—death itself. They said he was killed by a stray bullet. They said he fled from his house, so they killed him. They said he was walking along the road and so they shot him in the back. But after his death everyone disappeared. Even Alice vanished. I waited two years, but she had disappeared. Alice went to the Salonica Hotel to work as a maid, and the owner had a lot of affection for her. "She's a treasure," he said to me, winking with his left eye. At the time, I wasn't doing anything. I'd bring her a bottle of arak, get to the hotel, and see her sitting, waiting for me in the lobby among soldiers and men chewing their food and yawning. She'd take me to her room, and I'd see her trembling hands covered with black veins. When I'd pour her a glass, she'd slug it down in one gulp, the trembling would stop, and she'd start talking. I'd abandon myself to her words. She said I was like one of her children. "You're all my children," she'd say to me and everyone sitting around her. The owner would laugh, saying, "Not so, lady. We're not sons of a bitch!" and everyone would drown in laughter, and Alice would laugh. I would look at her and get scared. Who was this woman? I met Abd al-Karim by coincidence, but her, I don't know how I met her. Abd al-Karim, nicknamed Little Gandhi, was a shoe shiner. He never shined my shoes, but everyone had told me about him. I ran into him once and we talked for a long time. But her, I don't know, maybe another coincidence. She was a woman in her sixties, but there was nothing womanly about her—flat chest, an emaciated body that disappeared under her long black dress, eyes half-closed, a long nose, thin lips, and hands that constantly shook. She was a woman with nothing special about her, except that she reminds you of some other woman. It's always like that. We

3

give flight to our imagination when we see a woman, only because she reminds us of some other woman we used to know. Every woman has a female antecedent in our minds, and Alice was no exception. She looked like Victoria, the one crazy Antoun the garbageman would chase after, trying to kiss her because the store owner Emil promised him a lira if he could do it. Maybe I was fantasizing about Victoria, who I wanted to have, as did all the boys in the quarter, taking after their fathers. "All women are memories," I tried to say to Alice as she told me about Lieutenant Tannous. But she said no. She was right. In those days, I couldn't understand why she turned me down, because I was a coward. Now I know; all women are memories except the one that's potentially yours. For you're a man because you're some woman's potentiality. The woman who doesn't remind you of another one is your female potentiality. This one you don't fantasize about or with, this one kills you. You can't write her story because she takes you on the final journey to death.

Alice is the one who took me on the journey to Abd al-Karim and these names and faces. And now I ask, Who traveled and who remained? Did she take me on her journey and Abd al-Karim's journey, or was I just a mirror? I don't know. What I do know is that she traveled to Mosul and Baghdad and Aleppo before finally settling down in Beirut, whereas Abd al-Karim, otherwise known as Little Gandhi, never traveled at all. He stayed behind, attached to his wooden box, in front of the main gate of the American University. He stayed in Beirut and tried every possible occupation before dying on top of his box. But when he came to the end of his journey, Abd al-Karim didn't realize he'd traveled more than all the shoe shiners in the world. Not because he had come all the way from Mashta Hasan in Akkar to Beirut, but because Beirut itself travels. You stay where you are and it travels. Instead of you traveling, the city travels. Look at Beirut, transforming from the Switzerland of the East to Hong Kong, to Saigon, to Calcutta, to Sri Lanka. It's as if we circled the world in ten or twenty years. We stayed where we were and the world circled around us. Everything around us has changed, and we have changed.

Before he died, Abd al-Karim changed a lot. But death didn't give him a chance to see the city after it was transformed into its present Third World condition. Maybe it will happen to us too. Death won't give us a chance to see transformations we can't imagine. At any rate, the journey will end, whether we like it or not.

I'm the one narrating and writing. I want to travel with those people, but I find myself alone in a dark corner. I search for the rhythm of a journey that took place a few years ago, and feel like I'm digging in a deep well. I'm not digging, the well opens its mouth and pulls me in. And just as Abd al-Karim set out on his journey, and just as Alice, and Amin, and Malku, and Nuha, and Lillian, and Abu Saeed, and Rima and Husn and . . . set out on theirs, I, too, want to go. I discovered I was digging a well that was swallowing me up.

2

Alice said he died.

"I came and saw him, I covered him with newspapers, no one was around, his wife disappeared, they all disappeared, and I was all alone."

Alice said she took him to the cemetery, and she saw the people without faces. "People have become faceless," she told me. She spoke to them and didn't get any response, then she left them and went on her way. That's how the story ended.

"Tell me about him," I said to her.

"How shall I tell you?" she answered. "I was living as though I were living with him without realizing it. When you live, you don't notice things. I didn't notice, I just don't know." She shook her head and repeated her sentence. "All I know is, he died, and he died for nothing."

I recall Alice's words and try to imagine what happened, but I keep finding holes in the story. All stories are full of holes. We no longer know how to tell stories, we don't know anything anymore. The story of Little Gandhi ended. The journey ended, and life ended.

That's how the story of Abd al-Karim Husn al-Ah-

madi al-Mughayiri, otherwise known as Little Gandhi, ended.

Little Gandhi woke up. Little Gandhi didn't sleep a wink that night. It was unlike any of the nights of that strange summer. Beirut woke up as though it hadn't slept. There was salt. Everyone said the white salt had been sprinkled onto the streets, as though it had rained salt. But it hadn't rained, and the city was drowning in silence. Beirut was swimming in darkness and drowning. Little Gandhi felt as though the city was drowning. Silence climbed up the neck of the small man sitting alone in his usual corner in the cellar of the Burj al-Salam[1] building, which had been his home for the past six years. Little Gandhi was scared. Not the kind of trembling fear that pounded his back when he listened to the sounds of the planes attacking the city, a different kind of fear. Fear that seals your eyes shut, as if with two big stones. The small man couldn't open his eyes, but he didn't sleep. He'd see what looked like the shadow of his short, plump wife, pacing around the room as though she wanted to speak and didn't.

Suddenly it started, that roaring sound that tears door hinges apart.

Dozens of airplanes were circling low, sucking up the air and nearly touching the tops of the buildings. Little Gandhi didn't move an inch. It appears as though he did sleep, even though he thought he didn't. Sleep came to him in the middle of feeling wide awake, so he no longer knew whether he was seeing reality or dreaming. He opened his small eyes and didn't see anything. He found himself sitting

1. Burj al-Salam ("Peace Tower") was the highest skyscraper in Beirut and was occupied by several contending militias during the war.

in the corner of the room, right where he began. Fear devoured him. He leaned against the wall, and the wall felt like it was about to fall down. He opened his eyes and didn't see anything. He slept and didn't see anything. The darkness pierced by the whiteness of early dawn gave things a strange color. As he licked his lips with his tongue, his mouth filled with the taste of salt. Yesterday it rained salt. Little Gandhi saw the salt on the streets, saw that whiteness spread out as if it were the tongue of some dead animal stretching out into the streets.

"You are the salt of the earth," he said to the old Assyrian when he was at his store the night before. That was the fourteenth of September, 1982. The Israeli army was on the outskirts of Beirut, and the explosion in Ashrafiyyeh made him feel as though the city were going to fall into the sea. And he remembered the Reverend Amin, he remembered him as a young man standing in front of him with his white-and-brown shoes ready for polishing. Gandhi was confused about how to polish the perforated leather without upsetting the Reverend. He remembered the shoes and the Reverend's sallow, tawny face and white teeth as they spat out that expression he repeated endlessly: "You are the salt of the earth: but if the salt have lost his savour, wherewith shall it be salted?" The Reverend spoke with his teeth clenched. How will he speak later on, when he becomes senile and his teeth fall out? Little Gandhi saw the Reverend go senile and stop talking. He saw him in front of Our Lady of Lamentations Church, standing like a madman, saying nothing but Greek prayers. He remembered the Reverend and forgot his own name. He forgot why they named him Gandhi, for he didn't know who this man called Gandhi was. When the tall American professor told him Gandhi was a leader of India, and was a hero, Little Gandhi exploded with concealed laughter. Ever since he began working at Salim Abu Ayoun's restaurant, he didn't dare laugh, his laugh had become something like a yawn. The day before, when he heard the news of the explosion and the death of the president of the republic,[2] this very laugh came back to him. He left his laugh in front of Spiro with the hat's store and ran home.

The store owner, in his sixties, who always sat behind his desk swatting flies, was talking about the end of the war. And the old Assyrian was agreeing with him. Gandhi hated that Assyrian with the big nose, who bowed down to everyone. It's true he used to shine his shoes, and his childrens' shoes, but that all ended a long time ago. Little Gandhi had left the shoe-shining business five years earlier. It wasn't the first time he'd left his profession; he'd done so before when he opened a restaurant at the expense of the American dog. He talked about what happened with Mr. Davis, professor of philosophy at the American University of Beirut, who introduced him to the Reverend Amin and invited him to come pray at the church. Gandhi went only once to the church, but he became friends with Mr. Davis's dog, and through that friendship he became a restaurant owner.

Mr. Davis came to him once and asked him to help him feed his dog. "I don't have anything, all I have is shoes," Gandhi said.

But the American professor, who spoke Arabic with a real Beiruti accent, told him to get a burlap bag and follow him.

Gandhi followed him to the restaurant. He'd take the leftovers, put them in the bag, and then take them to Mr.

2. The bombing of the Phalangist Headquarters in Ashrafiyyeh, September 14, 1982, took the life of President-elect Bashir Jumayyil.

Davis's house. And from this bag he got his idea. He started bringing lots of bags with him. He'd give one bag to Davis's dog and take the rest to his house in Nabaa. There, in front of his house, he opened a restaurant. Labneh,[3] cheese, meat, kebab, hummus, vegetables, whatever. A plate of labneh, ten piasters, a plate of meat, half a lira, by God he actually opened a restaurant. Gandhi lived off of Mr. Davis's dog. When the dog died, he offered to buy Mr. Davis another dog. But Davis was very sad. They said he was going to divorce his wife, they said his wife killed the dog because she was jealous of him. But that didn't stop Gandhi from buying a German shepherd puppy and taking care of it in his house, causing the problems that almost drove his wife crazy and made Suad scream. And all of it for nothing, because Mr. Davis left, and the Reverend refused to take the dog, and the dog became attached to Gandhi, and Gandhi was forced to kill the dog and go back to shining shoes.

This time around, he left the business for good and got himself a better way to make a living, as the man responsible for keeping the quarter clean. Fawziyya, his wife, said he'd gone from being a shoe shiner to being a garbage collector. But that wasn't true. Now he was responsible for something; a garbage collector isn't responsible for anything. He sweeps the streets and picks up the trash and goes on his way. Little Gandhi, on the other hand, was responsible for the trash from A to Z. He had to distribute the plastic bags, pick them up, throw them away, and make sure no one violated the system.

They were sitting in front of the store discussing the end of the war. Little Gandhi was standing there, not be-

3. A strained yogurt paste eaten as a dip with bread.

cause he preferred to stand, but because he didn't know what he should do or say. He didn't sit down, he remained standing, listening to their chatter. The Assyrian talked about the cat food that went off the market during the long blockade, and Ms. Najat talked about the benefits of iodine from seawater, and Gandhi tried to understand why they were happy. He saw their faces elongate. The radio announced the bombing in Ashrafiyyeh and people began racing to their houses. Their faces became long, like masks. The masks ran in the city streets, and the streets became empty. Even the sound of people's footsteps was no longer heard. The storekeeper locked up his shop, Najat ran to her house, and Gandhi found himself walking along the city streets, not knowing where he was going. He understood this time that the war was not over. When he saw his son crying in the streets three weeks earlier, he thought the war was over. "The war is over," Gandhi had shouted, holding his son's shoulders as he took him home. His son's crying was a declaration of the end of the war. The Palestinian freedom fighters went to the sea, and the Israeli army was at the gates of Beirut.

"It's all over," his son said. "Before you know it, the tall American will be back, everything will come back, and we'll go back to the way we were."

Gandhi told his wife that night, after he'd fed his daughter Suad by forcing her to open her mouth and threatening to hit her while she ran away and held onto the walls and finally accepted, sitting like a chicken in front of him. He fed her as if he were stuffing her. She climbed onto the mattress on the floor and fell asleep. That day Gandhi told his wife that everything had gone back to the way it used to be, that his son the barber could go and start his life anew.

That day, the war became masks on people's faces. People became masks without eyes, walking like zombies through the city streets. Little Gandhi was walking. He didn't go to his house. Did he know he was going to die? And that he was taking his final walk? Is it true that people who are going to die smell death before it comes, and so they go toward it? Did Gandhi walk into his final good-bye when he stopped in front of the bar? He hesitated a long time before going in to find Alice in her usual place, standing beneath the dim red light, holding three red flowers. He didn't ask her where she disappeared to during the blockade. He himself didn't know anymore where he'd been, and he didn't remember anything from the days of the siege, except that he forgot everything. He forgot about people, and work. His wife told him he'd started going senile because he kept forgetting everyone's names. He didn't ask Alice anything. He came in and sat down behind the table in front of her. She served him a glass of brandy and he drank it down in one gulp. She laid her hand on his right hand, which he'd rested limply on the table, and started talking. Alice talked a lot. That's what Gandhi would've said if he'd told me the story himself. He'd have sighed about her talking too much and sat quietly. As for myself, my situation is different, since if it weren't for Alice and her talkativeness, I wouldn't have found out anything. But why did Gandhi tell her all those stories? Did he really tell her, or did she make them up and tell them as if they were true? She said she ran away from the Blow Up nightclub the day of the incident with Kamal al-Askary and Asad Awwad. You wouldn't know. She knew. She said the war began at the Blow Up, and for what reason? No reason. "My heart bleeds for them, they killed them, they killed the men and left the thugs." The day she fled, she met Little Gandhi, and he's the one who found her a job at the Montana on Hamra Street, next to the Burj al-Salam building.

If Kamal al-Askary hadn't died, then Alice wouldn't have met up with Gandhi, and if she hadn't met Gandhi, then he wouldn't have told her his story. And if Gandhi hadn't died, Alice wouldn't have told me the story. And if Alice hadn't disappeared, or died, then I wouldn't be writing what I'm writing now.

Alice held his right hand and tried to raise it up to her lips. Little Gandhi pulled his hand away. "Death is coming. Death is like salt."

"What kind of talk is this? Get up and go home to your wife and children."

"I know. I smell death," he said and got up.

She didn't ask him where he was going. She let him go and die. She knew, she said to me, she knew he was going to die. "He was afraid of death, and so he went to it, and died," Alice said to me, while the owner of the Salonica Hotel sat in front of us, his eyes roaming aimlessly about.

The man went home and tried to sleep. No one knew what he thought about that long night. Was he worried about his son Husn because he hadn't come home, or did he see his life pass before his eyes like a movie, as novelists say? What we do know is that he woke up early, feeling as if he hadn't slept at all. That's what Rima said he said. The roar of the airplanes rang in his ears. He made a cup of coffee, sweet, the way he liked it, and heard a faint knock at the door. His wife was asleep, and his daughter was tossing and turning in her bed as though she were awake. He opened the door and there was Rima, standing with her curly blond hair tied up on top of her head like a hat, hesitating to enter. She asked for Ralph, and when he told her he wasn't home, she wanted to leave. Gandhi invited her in for a cup of coffee, and told her his son hadn't slept at home, maybe he'd spent the night at the barber shop. It was as though she weren't hearing. She grumbled about the coffee being too sweet and then asked about the news. "The Jews are in Beirut," Gandhi said. "And Bashir Jumayyil is dead."

"Dead," she said in a soft voice and broke into tears. Everything in her cried. Gandhi wasn't sure, was she crying about the Jews, or because she was sad about the president's death? The way she cried was very strange. Her whole body shook, the cup of coffee slipped from her hands as she swayed as though she were dancing. She put the cup on the table and left quickly, her torso bent forward and her curly hair bouncing like a conglomeration of scattered blond strands on top of her head. Gandhi didn't try to stop her. He let her go and thought about his fate. He turned on the transistor radio and listened to the news of the Israelis entering Beirut. The sounds of explosions started. He didn't think about his son Husn, or his daughter sprawled on the floor, or about anyone. He thought about the shoe-shine box. He got up and hurried to the box, which had been thrown carelessly to the corner of the room, and began to clean it.

Gandhi was constantly thinking about Alice. Ever since that meeting, he'd felt as though he were personally responsible for her. Alice was strong enough. From the moment Gandhi took her to the Montana on Hamra Street, she'd been very independent. It's true that Hasan Zaylaa was the one who set up the whole thing, but Alice was able to adjust and ended up selling flowers in the bar. The clientele had changed; soldiers and groups of armed men came to the bar and swallowed their drinks as though they were drinking castor oil. Gone were the days of customers who sat and sipped their drinks, telling their stories and listening to stories about girls. Alice didn't like this new atmosphere, but she accepted it, and she managed to find some customers for her flowers and make a living for herself.

After two years of aimless hanging around because the Blow Up had shut down, Little Gandhi set her up at this bar, through the help of Zaylaa. Zaylaa was a story in himself. After he killed his oldest sister and tried to commit suicide, he joined one of the civil war organizations, and he migrated through all of the various organizations, ending up in charge of the bar department.

Alice used to say that his eyes oozed innocence despite his pale coloring and half-shaven beard, and his constant bragging about his criminal record. And in this bar Alice would meet Gandhi regularly, when he came almost every evening and drank a glass of brandy before going home. Alice couldn't forget Gandhi. "Even my own father I've forgotten, but not Gandhi. He was something else. He was a man . . . but somehow not a man . . . a man as if, how can I put it, as if you yourself are standing in front of a mirror. I know all kinds of men, from my father to those I met dancing in bars at age twelve, to that White Russian, what's his name? The one who used to sniff cocaine and dance on the table like a king, and he was a king, but they said he was an Israeli spy, these days everyone is an Israeli spy, but it's okay. And then there's the Lieutenant Tannous and his wife, and Abu Jamil the impresario, who bought and sold us, and then 'The Leader.'[4] I won't tell you about 'The Leader,' because you'll think I'm lying. Do I lie, my friend? After all, you're like my own son, and Gandhi, God rest his soul, was like my own son. I don't know what's

_____

4. "The Leader" is Abd al-Karim Qasim, who governed Iraq between 1958 and 1963.

wrong with me. Even The 'Leader,' when I grabbed him between his legs and he screamed, I thought of him as a son to me. I don't have any children, but when I remember them, I feel the milk is going to leak from my breasts. But the Reverend . . . the Reverend was different, he was a religious man, and with him I was different. I slept with him, the poor man forgot everything, imagine, he forgot he was a Reverend. He told me, Alice, my wife's name is Alice, but I didn't believe him. I took him through all the checkpoints to the nursing home in Ashrafiyyeh, and there the impossible happened, I'll tell you about that later. What was I saying? I was telling you something. I'm always talking about something. That's what the Lieutenant Tannous used to tell me, but he turned out to be a coward. Anyway, my son, what do you want me to tell you about?"

I'd listen to her and see her in front of me, but it was as though she weren't really there. She'd fade away into her words, as though her body vanished while the stories transformed into stories.

"Kamal al-Askary was a man, may God protect his honor, may God protect our honor. No one dared get close to him, that's why they killed him. They all killed him, left him there squirming in the bar. But poor Gandhi, or poor Abd al-Karim, I don't know why he had two names, as if he were more than one man. He was like a mirror. When he died, I felt as though the mirror had smashed to the ground, and it truly has fallen. And now, as you can see, flower selling is over for me. The owner of the Salonica Hotel is a disgusting man, I can't stand him. What have I become? A maid. If you only knew, my friend, how I used to be, but you don't know. You think that now is now, but it's not true, my son."

Alice ended her story with the scene of the dead man.

They found him lying on the road with the shoe-shine box next to him. They said he'd gotten scared. He heard the Israelis were arresting everyone, he was afraid of going to jail, he was afraid of going back to the cave they jailed him in a long time ago. He was afraid he'd be accused of cooperating with the freedom fighters, through his work in keeping the quarter clean. He was scared. He carried his shoe-shine box, hung it around his neck, letting it swing by its old leather strap, and he walked. And they were everywhere. They shouted at him to stop, or they didn't shout, no one knows. But they fired. They left him to fall on top of the box, his neck hanging from the rim, and his body slumped over.

Alice came and covered him with newspapers. She came from the bar where she'd slept that night. She'd heard the shots and came running. She saw him and saw the water that was falling on the city. She covered him. The salt that was spreading through the city melted in the rain-drops, and the papers covering him got wet and wrinkled. And Alice stood there in her long black dress, the rain pouring down on a city worn out by the siege.

"Everything that was, was a long time ago," Alice said. "You think I'm Alice, but it's not true, my son. Alice was, now means what was, and what was means a long time ago. And everything was a long time ago. There's no such thing as now."

Alice didn't say, she would disappear into streets littered with death. I searched for her a long time but didn't find her, as though she'd gone and entered into the destruction that had taken her.

3

Alice said he died.

"I came and saw him, I covered him with newspapers, there was no one around, his wife disappeared, they all disappeared, and I was all alone."

Alice said she took him to the cemetery, and she saw the people without faces. "People have become faceless," she told me. She spoke to them and didn't get any response, then she left them and went on her way. That's how the story ended.

"Tell me about him," I said to her.

"How shall I tell you?" she answered. "I was living as though I were living with him without realizing it. When you live, you don't notice things. I didn't notice, I just don't know." She shook her head and repeated her sentence. "All I know is, he died, and he died for nothing."

I recall Alice's words and try to imagine what happened, but I keep finding holes in the story. All stories are full of holes. We no longer know how to tell stories, we don't know anything anymore. The story of Little Gandhi ended. The journey ended, and life ended.

That's how the story of Abd al-Karim Husn al-Ah-

madi al-Mughayiri, otherwise known as Little Gandhi, ended.

Little Gandhi was born, he doesn't remember how, his father named him Abd al-Karim because he was called Husn, and his father had been Abd al-Karim, and his grandfather was Husn, and great grandfather was Abd al-Karim, and so on all the way back to Noah's Ark. But Noah, who fled to his ark, had no idea what might become of his descendants. You see, Noah and people like him who were able, and are able, to escape, have no idea that the real story is the one about those who couldn't escape. And since we all pretend to be runaways, for fear of being gobbled up by death, the stories about those who couldn't run away strike us as very odd, totally unbelievable. The stories seem distant, and we don't want anything to do with them, except merely as stories. Maybe this is what led me to my friendship with Abd al-Karim Husn al-Ahmadi al-Mughayiri, alias Little Gandhi.

I was standing in front of him with my shoe up on the footrest of his wooden box, thinking to myself, when I asked him what his name was.

"My name is Gandhi," he said.

"Welcome, Mr. Gandhi!"

I figured he must have been the son of an educated man from late Ottoman times, who lived during the days of the mandate and hoped to make his son a great leader for independence.

"It's a pleasure to meet you," I said to him, and then asked him where he was from.

"From Akkar."

"And was your father a shoe shiner, too?"

He smiled. "No. My father owns a store in the village, and he has some land and some goats."

I remembered the real Gandhi, and the goats with which he began his revolution against the British, and the stories of Haj Amin al-Husayni[5] when Gandhi presented him the goats as a gift. Everyone rejoiced then and said Palestine was liberated.

But Gandhi dashed all my hopes. His father didn't name him Gandhi, he named him Abd al-Karim, and he didn't call his son Nehru, instead he named him Husn. And his son didn't even like the name Husn, so he took the name Ralph when he was working in the barbershop, and with the onset of the war, he was confused about what he should do, so he called himself Ghassan, but the name didn't stick, so he went back to Husn and everyone laughed at him. Finally, he gave up and just let people call him whatever they wanted.

Rima called him Ralph, and his father called him Husn, and Madame Nuha called him Ghassan, and he responded to all three. As for Gandhi, it was Mr. Davis who gave him that name. He said he resembled Gandhi, and all the faculty from the American University started coming to take a look at him, and his name became Gandhi. If you ask him, he prefers people to call him Abu Husn, but no one calls him that. Even his wife, Fawziyya, doesn't call him anything but "man." Then he accepted the name when they added on the "little." That was thanks to the Reverend Amin. So then there was Gandhi of India and Little Gandhi, who was known to all the Ras Beirut locals by his sloppy gait and the wooden box hung around his neck. He was the only shoe shiner who hung his box from his neck. "It's like a noose," the Reverend Amin told him once. Gan-

5. Haj Amin al-Huseini was mufti of Jerusalem (1921), president of the Supreme Muslim Council in Palestine, and leader of the Palestine nationalist movement.

dhi laughed, or smiled, to be more precise, because he'd learned to conceal his laughter. He thought that death by hanging wouldn't be so bad. It wouldn't hurt, that's what Dr. Atef told him when he was asking him about it after witnessing the public hanging of Tannir. Now, this Tannir was known as a tough guy, but he made a mistake. He threw acid in the face of the woman he loved and then killed her husband. Her husband was a very well known lawyer, and so he was sentenced to death by hanging. How different he was from al-Askary, who was famous for his gallantry and high moral character. The problem wasn't with morals, it was with the rope. The difference between Tannir and al-Askary was that the first died by hanging, with everyone watching while he screamed and cursed everyone, saying that the woman had been cheating on him and her husband was an ass, and that he was the real victim. Whereas al-Askary died sprawled out on the floor of the Blow Up, left to squirm, no one bothering to pick him up. And when someone did pick him up, that was the end of it.

When Gandhi died, it was as though he'd been hanged by the strap of his shoe-shine box. Alice didn't dare untie the strap from his neck, because his clothes were drenched with water and were about to burst. Alice was afraid to go near him. She went and got some old newspapers, wrapped him in them, and began to scream.

Gandhi didn't remember many things about his childhood. When he tried to remember, standing next to his cousin at his father's funeral, he discovered he couldn't remember much about his village. To him, the village was a group of clay houses covered with white stuff. He came and didn't see the white stuff, all he saw were narrow, winding roads and faces he didn't recognize. But he cried anyway. He broke into tears while people looked on, watching him, as though the weeping of a son for his dead father had become something strange. Gandhi cried and didn't see anything. His cousin talked to him about how he should get married and Gandhi agreed, and decided he'd marry his cousin Fawziyya, and then he went back to Beirut. Gandhi wasn't sure how his relatives discovered Salim Abu Ayoun's restaurant, where he was working. He'd made up his mind to leave the restaurant, and the smell of dirty dishes, and the sound of Ms. Najat's moans, to work some other trade in which he could be free. His cousin came and took him to the village and back he came with Fawziyya. The moment he returned, he bought a shoe-shine box and sat near Jarjoura's Restaurant across from the American University and, with God's help, started to make a living.

Right after the burial, Gandhi went to the cave. He saw a small opening and smelled the scent of rotting bar- becued meat. He tried to go in, but he couldn't, because of the rocks and thorns and the stench. Here, in this cave, be- gan his family history. How often he thought about taking his daughter Suad there to bury her. But he feared God, he wasn't like Mr. Husn, who took him, grabbing him by the shoulder as if he were holding some mangy dog, and threw him there. Gandhi knew he'd made a mistake, but he never expected this kind of punishment. He was scared to death, and he discovered what it is like to have your feet become paralyzed and your tongue feel like a piece of rubber in your mouth. Here, in this cave, his grandfather's father died, and here he, too, was going to die. Everyone knew the story of his great grandfather, that's how the family name became "al-Mughayiri," "the Caveman." The crazy grandfather, whose name was Husn, went crazy in the cave and died there. The story goes that he went into the cave to kill the hyena that used to scare the villagers on winter nights. The hyena would come to this cave and sleep. The caveman grandfather entered, after swearing to all the young men in the village that he wasn't afraid. He waited for night to come and went in. They were watching him from the distance. Everyone said they didn't hear a sound from the cave, the man disappeared. He went in and didn't come back out. Three days later, he came out with his head crowned with white hair, his eyes were white, and he spoke without making sense. Everyone said Husn had gone mad, that the hyena terrified him, drove him crazy. After that the man stopped sleeping at home. Abd al-Karim, his son—that is, Little Gandhi's grandfather—told him that his father no longer slept at home, he slept out in the wild and howled like some rabid dog. A few months later, they found him dead in front of the entrance to the cave.

To this cave Husn took Abd al-Karim, his eleven-year-old son, and dumped him there.

"How can a father kill his own son?" Gandhi asked the Reverend Amin, who'd been trying to convince him to come to church and join in prayer.

"A father cannot kill his own son," the Reverend said. "He takes him to kill him, but there's always the lamb. Abraham took his son Isaac, you say Ismail, whatever, he took him because the lamb was there."

"And without the lamb?" Gandhi asked.

"Without the lamb, the world would've come to an end," he said. "Without the lamb, the father would've killed his son, and killed himself. God created the lamb for this purpose, the lamb is necessary for the existence of the father and the son."

"I get it, I get it, without the lamb it doesn't work," Gandhi said, getting back to work on the Reverend's shoes, which were full of brown holes.

"Of course, my son, you must come to church."

Gandhi didn't want to hurt that woman. He hated her, but he didn't really care. His father had come home, and she was with him. She had black hair, big eyes, she looked around as though she were frightened. People said his father had raped her in the woods and brought her to marry her. They said she was one of the nomads scattered around the Qummua forest, and the man had gotten involved with her and was afraid of her relatives, so he married her. She was the fourth wife, but she was number five, because Abd al-Karim's mother had died immediately after giving birth to him. Then he was unable to conceive anything but daughters from his other wives. Girls that filled the big house, and a sad man who didn't know what to do. Even this gypsy girl, who came from God knows where, gave him nothing but daughters.

Abd al-Karim was the only boy. He was sent to Qur'an school and learned the whole Qur'an by age seven. After that his father put him in the nuns' school in the village of Mashta Hammoud, an hour away from their village. Gandhi walked to Mashta Hammoud every morning, and when he returned home he was always afraid of the glances he would get from that woman who never stopped conceiving girls.

Gandhi didn't mean it, but she saw him. He'd swear today on the Holy Qur'an that he didn't mean it. But he didn't know why he froze in his place. He went to the fields to urinate, then he started. The sun was starting to go down, and the scene of the yellow fields in summer blocked the horizon with piles of wheat waiting to be threshed, and Gandhi stood, imagining the scene of the nun bending down in front of his desk to pick up the chalk that had fallen on the floor. His eyes disappeared behind his eyelids and his hand began to roam around the nun's black robe, and he lost himself inside her dress, not wanting to come back out. Along came that woman, she appeared out of nowhere, and started hitting him with a long olive branch. As she was hitting him, he held onto his penis with a strange ecstasy, as if his body no longer belonged to him. Little Gandhi didn't know why he didn't stop. He tried to turn around so the woman couldn't see what was in his hand, while she kept circling around him, hitting him. And when the world crumbled between his hands, he saw her standing there in utter shock, the branch in her hand, staring with two huge eyes and her mouth half open. All of a sudden, she threw the branch and ran away. He, too, ran off to the house and sat alone, trembling. She disappeared.

That night his father grabbed him by the shoulder and took him to the cave. His father didn't say a word, and neither did Abd al-Karim. He walked along with shaky feet wherever his father ordered him to go, and he heard his father saying something like he deserves to die. Abd al-Karim was convinced he was going to die, but he didn't. Now, when he would tell the story to Alice, he'd nearly get his story in the cave mixed up with his grandfather's. He'd tell the story of his father's wife, and then the story of the hyena, to the point where he was sure he was the main character in both stories.

Abd al-Karim didn't sleep in the cave that night. He was overcome with fear and cold. It was the middle of summer and yet he felt the cold gobbling him up. He didn't know where he got the courage to do it, but he ran away. He walked the whole night out in the fields, thinking he was going toward Syria, but after three days of walking and never-ending stories, he wound up in Tripoli. There, in Tripoli, his journey began. From Tripoli to Beirut, from the bakery, to the restaurant, to the shoe-shine box, and from Nabaa to Ras Beirut.

In Tripoli, he worked at Master Rashid's bakery. Master Rashid knew who he was and gave him a job in his bakery. And there he was engulfed with warmth: fire, warmth, and the aroma of baked bread, and the round loaves, round as the full moon. In the bakery, his fear of the cave came back to him. Night in the bakery was scary. Gandhi was afraid of sleeping upstairs next to Master Jafar with his big belly and beard and the sweat that dripped relentlessly from his body. Master Jafar was in front of the oven, the flames flashing in his eyes even as he slept. He'd eat and eat, as if he never got full, and sleep in the bakery, because he wasn't married. Gandhi was scared of Jafar, scared of his snoring and questions about sex. Gandhi was afraid. He'd listen to the advice of Mrs. Rashida, Master Rashid's wife, as she served him a bite of what she was cooking, to nourish his skinny body.

Gandhi loved Tripoli and he loved fish.[6] But after three long years spent between the upstairs room, the deaf woman's house, and delivering bread to customers' houses, he decided to pack up and go to Beirut. Life in the bakery had become unbearable, and Master Rashid was never the same after his wife died. When Master Rashid asked him to learn to work the ovens, Little Gandhi felt he just couldn't anymore. He decided to leave his job and go to Beirut. Without a good-bye to anyone, he picked up his things and off he went to Beirut, in search of Ms. Najat's Restaurant. Ms. Najat, who used to visit her family in Tripoli from time to time, told him to come whenever he wanted, for a different kind of job. So he went, and in her restaurant he found out what it was to be alone, and how

6. Tripoli is the second largest city in Lebanon, located on the sea and famous for its fresh fish markets.

to live in the cold. Six years of cold and fear, things went on around him as if he didn't see any of them. Little Gandhi told Alice that he wasn't aware of things. He'd read bits of news from the papers wrapped around the loaves of bread, and he'd go to the movies, and see the customers, but he wasn't aware. The fear that swallowed him in the cave at Mashta Hasan came with him to Tripoli, as he stood in front of the oven-cave of the bakery. Then this same fear took him to Beirut, to Najat's moans and the pain in his knees that was to stay with him his whole life. He didn't realize he'd started to see things until he came back from the village with Fawziyya and bought the shoe-shine box. Then Little Gandhi understood the meaning of life. He told his wife he had to get his head together. Life is what's in your head, he said. He carried his head in his hands and set off for the entrance to the American University. He knew that working in the Nabaa area would be impossible, since poor people don't have their shoes shined, and in the Burj area it would be expensive, because you have to pay half your salary to the thug protecting you. In front of Jarjoura Restaurant, however, you could sit and watch the AUB girls and live a nice life. True, the money wasn't very good at first, but times changed and things got better.

Gandhi was afraid of death. Fawziyya would get pregnant, give birth, and then the baby would die. Four babies died, until Suad came and survived, and after her Husn lived, but with difficulty, thanks to Dr. Davis. For fear of risking Fawziyya's health, the doctor ordered him to use condoms, and that's another story. Then Fawziyya stopped getting pregnant, and Gandhi was relieved from death and condoms and got back to his work. He was trying to save some money to move from Dahr al-Jamal in Nabaa to Hamra Street, but the money didn't hold out. Even when his restaurant was at its peak, he couldn't save even one piaster.

Alice believed money does not last.

Alice used to tell him poor people's money is like salt that melts in your hands, and evaporates with the water. She'd carry on with her never-ending memories, from Lieutenant Tannous to "The Leader," and Gandhi would smile.

"You, my dear, are partial to officers."

"Officers are the best," Alice would answer. "You, what do you know. When an officer, with all his stars and stripes, bends down on the ground at your feet, and cries out in pain, and even better, when those stars themselves squirm in pain right before your eyes, it is then that you see the world as a totally different place. But everything is gone, even the money's gone. Now look what's become of me."

Alice always loved to tell the story of Lieutenant Tannous, because when he left and his wife was standing at the door, he cried. He went back to her once, but she kicked him out, she slept with him and then kicked him out. As for "The Leader," that's another story.

At that time Alice was working at the Mirabelle Bar on Rawshi Street, when the impresario Abu Jamil came along. He knew Alice had suffered after Lieutenant Tannous left her. Abu Jamil came early in the morning and took her home with him. He placed a bottle of cognac in front of him and started drinking and talking. He told her about the "great deal." "The best deal, Alice, is Mosul. You've been to Aleppo, but Mosul is totally different, Brits and army men and money, you can have anything you want. There's a group going in two weeks, for one month, the salary is two thousand liras a week, not including tips, all expenses paid. Just say the word . . . "

The room was pitch black.

They told her that's what the man had said. You go into the room and don't turn on the lights, climb onto the bed naked, and after that he'll come. He didn't say who he was, he said he'd come, and don't open your mouth.

The man waited for her outside. Alice was tired, for the third day in the Big Mosul Club had been exhausting. Englishmen and champagne bottles popping in the air, and the Greek woman from Beirut capturing their hearts, while Alice sat semi-isolated, feeling weak in the knees every time she stood up. When she'd go over to the customers' tables and sit, her body would tense up. The hands pawing at her feet and thighs there were different, as though the fingers got stuck to her flesh and tore her. Alice felt she'd failed in Mosul. Anita, the Greek girl, was the winner this time. It had been Alice who had stolen the hearts of the commanders at Mirabelle in Beirut, with her laughter and hoarse voice and fading olive complexion. Here, she felt lonely and undesirable, as though they didn't want anything to do with her dancing or her dimples or her big eyes.

At two o'clock in the morning, the man came and took her. She left the club without being noticed by anyone, to find herself in a black room. The curtains were drawn and she could smell Indian incense. At first she couldn't see anything, then the darkness began to give way to a wide bed and a chair and a table. She took off her clothes and hung them over the chair and climbed onto the bed. She waited a long time. It seems she fell asleep. She woke up to a hand caressing her neck. She could smell a man, but saw nothing, and when she tried to speak, he put his hand over her mouth without saying a word. She was silent and let him do what he wanted. He had all of his clothes on, he didn't even take off his shoes. He kissed her on her left cheek. His lips moved down and he moved down, and he collapsed between her feet. He stayed there a long time, and Alice got scared. The trembling of her thigh muscles extended to every corner of her body. There he was, he smelled like a combination of dust and salt. When he came up again and took hold of her breasts, she tried to turn in his direction to kiss him, but he pushed her away and turned his back to her. And so Alice went back to her first position, naked, and alone, and flat on her back. Alice kept quiet, left him to do what he pleased and shut her eyes. She tried to sleep. After a short while he came back to her, got on top of her and put his hands on her breasts, kissed her, and then seemed to want to sleep. He put his head on her stomach and didn't move. Then he started pinching her all over her body. She moaned without crying out, the pain rippling down between her shoulders. Something of Mary Naquz had come back, something of that sexual pleasure Alice had known only once in her life and refused to repeat again afterward. The experience had come to her. The man, with all his clothes on, would move around her in the dark, then he'd settle down while she trembled, alone. She tried to take hold of his hand and put it on her chest, but the hand pulled away. He came close to her and flooded her with his whole body, then turned his back and went to sleep.

Alice didn't sleep that night. She was waiting for dawn, but it didn't come. She wanted to sleep with a man, but this man had fallen into a deep sleep. Alice dozed off without realizing it, and when she woke up, she found the same darkness. She got up and tried to open the door, but it was locked with a key. She tried to open the curtains, but they wouldn't open. She went back to the bed and fell asleep again. After a while, she didn't remember how long, the door opened and the man from the day before came in with a battery-powered lamp. He asked her to get dressed and follow him. She got dressed and followed. He took her through endless corridors. The day before she hadn't noticed these corridors, maybe because she'd drunk so much champagne, and today she didn't notice when the dark man had left her, maybe because she'd fallen asleep. When they reached the door, the man gave her an envelope full of money and told her the driver would take her to the hotel, and things were set for tomorrow. When Alice got to the hotel, Abu Jamil didn't dare ask her anything or ask for his cut. The agreement was that she'd pay him fifty percent of the tips. She went to her room and slept until evening. The next day, the same story; three weeks, and every day, the same story.

The last day, when the man with no features was half asleep, Alice sat on the bed and said she was leaving the next day. She thought she heard the word *fine,* in a Syrian accent, come out of his mouth, but she wasn't sure whether it was he who was talking or a dog barking outside. He said only one word, and that night he pinched her a lot, until her body was covered with bruises, causing her to have to stay home from work for a whole week when she got back to Beirut.

When that dark man left, all memory of him went along with him. Alice forgot him and went back to work at Mirabelle. She'd spot Lieutenant Tannous on the other side of the cabaret, not daring to go near her. She'd smile at him and he'd leave, then she'd go back to listening to people's stories and being shocked by these tragedies hidden deep within their paunches.

Two years later, Abu Jamil came to offer her the same opportunity: Mosul. Alice hesitated a lot, while Abu Jamil rubbed his hands and went on about how the door of opportunity was open and the man never stopped asking for her. Alice hesitated, remembering that frightful darkness in Mosul. She remembered being afraid, and how the man used to climb her as if she were a tree, not a woman. But she went anyway. And once again, for a whole month, she was enveloped by an endless darkness, from which she didn't know how she escaped.

That's how things are.

"The horses were green," Gandhi said.

Little Gandhi was unable to forget the green horses. They trampled over men's backs, and the men moaned. It was called al-Mashayikh Thursday. And there was the child who could see from only one eye; he'd wander among the men's feet, trying to see. The horses would appear between the men's feet, green in color. Little Gandhi had never seen green horses anywhere except on al-Mashayikh Thursday. When he asked the Reverend Amin about them, he laughed and patted his back. "You are naive," he said, and then something from the Bible about those who inherit the earth. "Blessed are the meek, for they shall inherit the earth."

"What do you mean by blessed, Reverend?" Gandhi asked.

"Blessed means how lucky they are. How lucky you are, Gandhi, because you saw the green horse. No one but John the Baptist has ever seen that horse."

"Send my best to John the Baptist, Your Highness."

The green horses flowed between their feet while the men lay prostrate and the sheikh mumbled and moaned. He sat alone on a high bench, the scene taking place all around him. A man rose up from under the horses' hooves and ran toward the sheikh, kissed his hand, and wept. This is what Husn, the father of Abd al-Karim Gandhi, used to do. He'd lie flat on the ground and the green horses would trample over his back, then he'd get up, crying, and go toward the sheikh. The tears would stay in his eyes for three days, hanging from his eyes like small drops of crystal, swaying between his eyelids without falling. When the man died and Gandhi came to the village and entered the room where he was laid down, wrapped in white shrouds, he didn't see the tears in his eyes. They were closed, and black, like two small stones. That day Gandhi wept. He didn't know where his love for this man who had wanted to kill him in the cave had come from. All of a sudden, he felt this man was his father, that it had been a stranger in Mashta Hasan.

After the funeral, his cousin took him aside and talked to him about Fawziyya. This cousin, who lived in Tripoli, said he'd waited a long time for him to come and that the girl must get married, and that he's more entitled to marrying her than anyone else.

Gandhi nodded his head in agreement, and his uncle took his right hand and said, "Let's read *al-Fatiha*."[7] They read *al-Fatiha* and a month later, when Gandhi returned to the village to be married, his father's wife, the one with the black hair, that gypsy who'd sent him to the cave, told him that he could live in the house. But he didn't want to. All he wanted was to finish with the wedding quickly and get back to Beirut. The wedding took place with the least possible expense—lemonade and sugar and a single ululation from his father's wife. He took Fawziyya and went back to Beirut, and from that day on he never returned to the village. Well, no, he did go back to Mashta Hasan for Suad's sake. They'd told him the sheikh could cure her. Gandhi went to him with his young daughter and her confused eyes, scrawny body, and her broken speech. The sheikh sat her down in front of him in a dark room, full of the smell

7. Al-Fatiha is the opening sura of the Qur'an, customarily read at social occasions such as marriage contracts, visiting the dead, and so on.

of incense and the sound of mysterious words. The sheikh asked for fifty liras and gave Gandhi an amulet, but his daughter didn't get any better. Actually, her state worsened, and if not for God's mercy, they'd have killed her.

"The crazy girl ran away to Nabaa by herself." Gandhi said this was God's mercy; if it hadn't been for that mercy, she'd have gone and died in her shame. "The medicine was no longer available," Gandhi told Alice. "She became, I don't know how, she'd walk around and bang on the walls, and then she just disappeared. I said to myself, it's all over for you, Gandhi. The girl won't be crazy anymore, but she'll die. If they haven't killed her, you will."

Gandhi didn't kill his daughter. Suad came back three days later looking exactly the same, as though nothing had happened. Maybe if they'd raped her she'd have gotten better, Gandhi thought. She came back home as though she'd never left. Only she stuttered a little more and spoke incomprehensibly.

"She speaks like a lunatic, come and hear her," Gandhi said to Ralph.

Ralph wasn't interested. He'd come home tired. He sat next to his sister and listened to her, then started laughing. The young girl told her story to everyone, but no one understood a word. Was it true they took her to a garage and tried to rape her, but one of them started vomiting and trembling, so they left her and ran away? Or is the real story that Tino, that was the leader's nickname, it seems, Tino told them to leave her alone because she was crazy and she'd give them God only knows what kinds of diseases? Or was it that Michalany, "what the heck is his name—the one who saved me—Shali, yes, Shali," was it Shali or Michalany who started banging his head against the wall and shouting, "Leave her alone, I won't allow it, I . . ."

and took her out of the garage and brought her to Museum Square?

No one really knew what happened to the girl when she fled to their old house in Nabaa, in East Beirut, and came back the same way she left.

"Even those armed men, those sons of bitches, didn't touch her. I told my cousin, please take her, take her for one day, and then if you don't want her, send her back. The only thing that can cure her is for a man to sleep with her and make her bleed. But the son of a bitch refused. I told him, you can send her back, no questions asked, I'll pay. But he was afraid. He, too, was afraid. And what's wrong with the girl, she's beautiful. He's a son of a bitch, he smells, and he refused. He said he didn't want to get married, does anyone refuse marriage? He said his wife won't allow it. Does anyone refuse to marry a second wife?"

The girl returned, and Little Gandhi returned from his attempts to find a cure for her, void of all hope. His wife said, "This is our fate, my dear, we have to be content with it. Contentment is a treasure." And so Gandhi was satisfied with his treasure and stopped searching.

Gandhi told the Reverend Amin the story, but he didn't understand any of it. He looked at Gandhi with clouded eyes and snored, as though he were asleep. Gandhi felt sorry for the Reverend. He'd pass by him at his house on the second floor of that building, which was painted purple like a piece of hard candy. Those days Gandhi would go to the Reverend and give him bread, and some money. And the Reverend seemed to be unconscious; if it hadn't been for Alice, he'd have been left to die, paralyzed on the steps of the Church of the Virgin on Makhoul Street.

Gandhi could remember the Reverend in his younger days. That was just after he'd come to Beirut, in the middle of the crisis with the dog. After Mr. Davis's dog died, Gandhi went back to his original profession. He got the shoeshine box and sat in front of the American University. He took the Reverend's advice on his new plan and bought a dog to replace Fox and named it Fox. He tried to persuade Mr. Davis, but Mr. Davis just couldn't understand. He'd walk all alone on Bliss Street, in front of the university, unable to speak.

John Davis said his mission in Lebanon had failed.

He said he came and became a real Arab, he loved the people, loved Beirut, loved fried fish and cauliflower with tahini sauce, he loved them and became one of them. But it was impossible. The East is barbaric; if not for India and the real Gandhi, the East would've remained barbaric.

John Davis couldn't understand how that man had laughed at him as he knelt trembling over his dead dog.

"It's a dog, sir, just a dog," the man said, and then he spit.

It wasn't enough that he'd killed the dog, the man had to spit on him, because dogs are filthy.

It was then that Davis cut off his relationship with the Reverend Amin. The Reverend tried to lessen the blow for Davis by helping Gandhi raise the dog for the sake of his American friend, and for the sake of their friendship, but the American professor couldn't take the shock, and couldn't understand how the Reverend had spoken in defense of the Arabs and rejected what he'd said. Their friendship was famous. The Reverend Amin would speak to him in English, with a New York accent that he didn't really know, and Davis would respond with his own unpolished Beiruti Arabic. Davis was studying moral philosophy at the American University, and the Reverend Amin was in charge of the Beirut parish of the Episcopal church. Both were Protestants. The Reverend Amin believed that

America was the heart of civilization and progress and freedom, and Mr. Davis detested New York, where he'd lived and taught in its universities, and loved the East and spices and Arabs. Mr. Davis's story is unusual, especially when he tells how he learned Arabic from Mustafa Ghalayini, the barber, before studying it in Shimlan, at the school that was founded solely for teaching Arabic to foreigners. Mr. Davis, who'd lived alone with his wife, with no children, left Beirut seven years before the beginning of the civil war in 1975. And it appears that the murder of his dog was decisive in deciding his future. Mr. Davis told the Reverend Amin that he felt extremely lonely, and that all his work in Lebanon was a complete loss.

"Suddenly I feel like a stranger, I feel that no one, no one in the world cares for me. And my wife, who's constantly sick, wants to go back to the States. This is my country, but I'm going. All has failed. I'm not upset about the dog, but how could he have spit on him? How?"

The American professor bent over his dog, who was in the throes of death in the middle of the street, and the driver who'd run over him with his car got out of the car and spat. The professor felt that everything had come to an end, and nothing the Reverend Amin tried did any good, including helping Little Gandhi take care of Fox's replacement, which Gandhi bought, making sure it was of the same breed as the original Fox.

When the professor refused to take the dog and Gandhi wanted to get rid of it, Lillian suggested killing it. And it was the Reverend who went to the drugstore and bought the poison that Gandhi put in the dog's milk.

Little Gandhi didn't like the Reverend Amin, for, in spite of his kindness and that of his parishioners, he was haughty. He spoke with a low voice and used a dialect that was a cross between Beiruti colloquial Arabic and classical

Arabic, and he was always shaking his head to give the impression he was trying to understand others. But then he'd turn around and do whatever made him feel good. The smell of whiskey was always on his breath, and the stories of his adventures with Lillian Sabbagha were well known, or they'd become well known, after Madame Sabbagha disclosed them during one of her crazy spells. That was when her Russian maid Vitsky Novicova died. She stood in front of the maid's room with a handkerchief over her mouth and started screaming. Then she cursed the Reverend Amin and divulged all their secrets.

Gandhi became interested in the Reverend Amin because he felt sorry for him. His wife left him and joined their children in the United States, and he suffered a total breakdown. The Reverend started wetting his pants and speaking nonsense. Every morning he'd go to the Church of the Virgin, stand in front of an icon of the Virgin, make the sign of the cross, and bow down so low his forehead touched the ground, then he'd stand like an idiot in front of the Royal Door. He'd raise his hands to the heavens and approach the altar. And Father John would take him aside, set his mind at ease, and remind him he was a minister and it was his duty to watch over his parish. But it appeared that the Reverend Amin had forgotten everything. He forgot about his parish, and that he was a Protestant, and no longer remembered any prayers except for one sentence: *"Doxa patri kai huio kai hagio pneumati nun kai aei kai eis tous aionas ton aionon.* Amen." "Glory to the Father and to the Son and to the Holy Spirit, now and forever and unto ages of ages. Amen."

Senility, Father John would say, thanking Alice for her kindness. "My child, you are a good woman, may God have mercy on you in your old age."

The Reverend Amin lost track of everything. He forgot he was married and had children and no longer knew anything but a few prayers in Greek. He forgot the story of his grandmother, Um Tanios, in Sidon, who would yell "O Muhammad, my beloved." And he forgot how he became a minister in return for a favor the Reverend Salim extended to his father during the war, when he saved him from starvation by appointing him a professor in the School of Art in Sidon. And so his father became a Protestant, but never got over the habit of making the sign of the cross.

The Reverend forgot everything, even Madame Sabbagha, whom he wished would fly. He used to tell her she was incapable of flying, because she was a worthless woman, and that he'd loved her because, he'd discovered, he was no good with women. He forgot everything, and he'd been cast aside, alone, in front of the Church of the Virgin, with no one to care for him, in the middle of the bombs of war that fly and transform the city into a desert of lost faces. When Alice took him to the nursing home in Ashrafiyyeh, he couldn't speak. He was standing in front of the church, with some militia men around him who were making fun of him. He was like a stray animal, smelling dirty, unshaven, his hands clinging to the church banister so he wouldn't fall down.

Alice took him home, cleaned him up, dressed him in clean clothes, and fed him. She got a taxi and took him to East Beirut, to the nursing home in Ashrafiyyeh.

Sister Efdukiya, who was sitting behind her desk, all covered in black robes with nothing showing but a round white face full of peroxide-bleached white hairs and a wart under her nose with three black hairs growing out of it, refused to take the man in. She said she wanted money. "Please, Sister. I beg you. The man is all alone and doesn't have anyone. And, after all, he's a Christian and you're obligated to take care of him."

"Impossible," the nun answered.

The Reverend Amin wept. It was as though a piece of his memory had come back to him, or as if he'd seen himself in the mirror. He wept and made the sign of the cross and shouted *"Doxa patri kai huioi."* But neither his weeping nor his prayers did any good with Sister Efdukiya, so Alice paid 1000 liras and told her she'd pay the first of every month.

Alice bent over the Reverend's hand and kissed it and went back to Beirut.

She went back and told Gandhi. She told him all her stories, except for the officer's moment of madness. "The officer went crazy. He wasn't just an officer, he was a leader, he might have become president."

Alice didn't know how they allowed her to leave that place. But Gandhi didn't believe her, and neither did I.

4

Alice said he died.

"I came and saw him, I covered him with newspapers, there was no one around, his wife disappeared, they all disappeared, and I was all alone."

Alice said she took him to the cemetery, and she saw the people without faces. "People have become faceless," she told me. She spoke to them and didn't get any response, then she left them and went on her way. That's how the story ended.

"Tell me about him," I said to her.

"How shall I tell you?" she answered. "I was living as though I were living with him without realizing it. When you live, you don't notice things. I didn't notice, I just don't know." She shook her head and repeated her sentence. "All I know is, he died, and he died for nothing."

I recall Alice's words and try to imagine what happened, but I keep finding holes in the story. All stories are full of holes. We no longer know how to tell stories, we don't know anything anymore. The story of Little Gandhi ended. The journey ended, and life ended.

That's how the story of Abd al-Karim Husn al-Ah-

madi al-Mughayiri, otherwise known as Little Gandhi, ended.

As Alice stood amidst the salt and water that drenched the papers she covered Little Gandhi's body with, Rima was standing on the corner across the street. Alice didn't see Rima and she didn't recognize her. Rima had met her once at Little Gandhi's house, but she didn't remember her, nor did she remember that meeting, when Ralph came in with that blond girl, who spoke with long pauses between her words. Alice didn't pay any attention to her at the time, in spite of the fact that the girl had come especially to meet her. Ralph had spoken a lot about Alice, and she wanted to meet her and find out about that strange world hiding underneath the crust of Beirut.

Rima used to tell Ralph she didn't know anything. How would she know. Even her love for this young man, who worked as a barber in Joseph Tabshurani's salon behind Maqdisi Street in Hamra, was uncertain. He told her about his relationship with Madame Nuha. She used to smell it on his body when he'd slept with her, that thirst for the other woman. It was as though he clung to her to keep himself from falling. "Love is not like that," she said to him once. But she was in love with him, or wanted to be in love with him, for after her experience with Hassan, and that feeling that a dreadful chasm had opened up inside her, she decided never to go back to that pit. With Ralph, the pit was nonexistent. There was a kind of silence that enveloped her body. When he came close to her, she felt there was a distance separating him from her, and this distance bothered her sometimes, but it gave her a strange kind of safety. With Hassan, it had been different. She had met him five years earlier in the emergency room of American University Hospital, where she'd come with a group of people who were living in Abi Haidar Tower, to bring a wounded man who'd been hit by some stray bombs. And there started this strange relationship that was impossible to stop. Hassan was different from her. He was from the village of Ayn Unoub in the Aley area. Every weekend he'd go to his village, where he said he felt he belonged. He lived on Verdun Street, but slept in the hospital three nights a week. In two years he was to graduate and go to the States to do his specialization in gynecology. Rima, on the other hand, felt she wasn't from anywhere. Her father lived in Italy, where he worked for a big pharmaceutical company, and her elderly German mother never stopped drinking whiskey and swearing. Her mother, whom her father divorced after ten years of marriage, with Rima being the only fruit of that marriage, was quickly approaching her death. She couldn't bear marriage and she couldn't bear divorce. She fell in love with a man nine years younger than she, and when he married her, she hated him, and turned his life into a living hell. And now she was living in hell. After he divorced her and fled to Italy, this woman, who was nearly sixty years old, became half-crazy. "My mother is half-crazy," Rima said to Hassan as she told him how she no longer understood her feelings toward her mother and her émigré father and this city she was born in.

At home, Rima spoke German with her mother, and at work, at the Mediterranean Bank, she spoke French, and with her friend the doctor, Arabic. She didn't know how to speak anymore, as if she'd forgotten the three languages she knew, and started giving this strange impression that she was putting spaces between her words. She'd stop talking in the middle of a sentence, as if she were searching for the right word, or she'd forgotten what she wanted to say. Rima, who'd fled from her mysterious relationship with Hassan, found herself trapped in an even more mysterious relationship with Ralph, or Husn, or Ghassan. The young man with the three names appeared to be more than one person. He slipped between her hands, he seemed strange, as if she didn't know him. Indeed, she didn't know him. She met him by chance. She's the one person in this novel who wasn't living or working in Hamra, or specifically on Maqdisi Street, and the streets branching from it leading to Bliss Street. Rima was living with her mother in Abi Haidar Tower and felt entirely out of place in Beirut. She came back from France in 1976, because she could no longer stand living alone, and took a job in the Mediterranean Bank, so she wouldn't be without work. She fell in love with Hassan because he was the first one in this strange city who appeared to her to be a man. She didn't know what it was she saw in him, because there was nothing very special about him. He had a big nose, thick eyebrows, and arms that seemed shorter than most people's. He was neither short nor tall, fat nor thin, and in spite of all this she fell into a semimagical relationship with him. From the first day they met, and after he'd finished caring for the wounded man, whose name Rima didn't know, though she'd brought him and others to the hospital because she happened to be standing on the balcony when the bomb landed, and so she ran to the street and found herself in the hospital, the doctor looked at her, sweat dripping from his forehead, and asked her to buy him a cup of coffee. They went to L'Express and from there to his house. She smoked hashish, got drunk, and laughed. Then she started going almost every night, to smoke with the same group. She found out that Hassan had been involved with every one of the young women she saw at his house. At first she wasn't upset, but then she began to feel that chasm taking form in her chest. When she'd meet with Hassan, she would feel as if she couldn't breathe; this strange world this doctor had taken her to made her lose all feeling of herself. She'd sit on the couches that were lined up in the living room, smoke and drink, and listen to music, while he sat there, seemingly unconscious, but she couldn't bear to live without him. She thought of asking him to marry her, but she got his answer before even asking the question. She could hear it in his boisterous laughter and carefree talk. Rima didn't know a lot about him. He said he was involved in the fighting at the beginning of the war, but then he became disgusted, this place is disgusting, heading for extinction, he'd go to America and never come back.

Rima was afraid. When Ralph came and told her, she didn't believe him. Then she started throwing up. His eyes bulged and there was a razor-sharp coldness in his voice. He said he'd killed the woman, and he wanted to marry her. "Now I can marry you."

He followed her to the bathroom, where she stood in front of the sink, vomiting. He embraced her from behind, as though he wanted to make love to her. Everything in her insides flowed over as he held her waist, forcing her toward him. Then he collapsed onto the toilet and sat motionless. She left the bathroom and went into her bedroom, and heard her mother's voice, in German, asking her what was going on. Then Ralph followed her to her bedroom, sprawled out onto the floor, and fell asleep.

Rima couldn't believe he'd killed Madame Nuha. He didn't tell anyone he killed her. He told his father he came home and found her dead. He said he left the house key inside, went out, and shut the door behind him, but he didn't know anything.

"Let's call an ambulance," Gandhi said.

"No, no. She's already dead," said Husn.

Gandhi didn't say a word. He knew it was his son who'd committed the murder, but he didn't ask. Then Husn went out. He yelled to him, and this time he called him "Husn," and his son answered. He came back, sat down, and lit a cigarette, but Gandhi didn't ask him anything. When they broke down the door to his house, after the neighbors began smelling the stench of the rotting corpse, they saw Madame Nuha Aoun with torn clothes, her body bloated, and her three cats around her, also dead. Everything in the house was locked—the doors, the windows, the shutters—and the woman was there on the floor, and the three cats, dead. They took her to the hospital for an autopsy before burying her. No one attended the funeral. The Reverend Amin was there, all alone, muttering prayers and fearing this kind of end. Everyone said Husn was the murderer, but comrade Abu Karim put his mind at ease. He said don't worry about it, "She has no relatives, and no one's going to ask about her." But Rima became fearful of Ralph. He told her not to call him Ralph ever again, that his name was now Ghassan, and she should call him Ghassan, and so she did. When she slept with him, she'd get that sour feeling that gnashed at her insides, precisely the way she felt when she slept with Abu Abd al-Kurdi, the concierge of the building where Hassan lived. She didn't choose to sleep with him; it had never crossed her mind. She was on her way out from Hassan's house, going down the dark stairs from the third floor, where he lived. There was no electricity and Rima hadn't lit a match. As she went down the stairs, in the dark, she felt as though she were swimming in a swamp, with bugs swarming all around her. She saw him, she saw his swaying shadow. He was climbing the stairs carrying a long white candle, his shadow swayed past the stairs, giving the impression he was falling to the ground. He reached out as if to stop her, and Rima bumped into his arm, nearly falling down. He grabbed her by her waist with his outstretched hand and pulled her toward him. Rima didn't say anything. She remembers that she said no, she said tomorrow, but he didn't say anything. He rammed her with his head and forced her to the ground. Rima fell on the stairs, and there he took her. He didn't take off his pants, he entered her with all his clothes on, after lifting her short skirt. Everything happened quickly, and Rima felt that sourness rise to her throat. He got off of her, pants and all, walked away, and left her on the stairs, as though he hadn't done anything, and continued up the stairs. After that, every time Rima went down the stairs, it seemed as though she were waiting for him, and she actually was. With him she felt free, she felt she could liberate herself from this Hassan whom she visited on a daily basis. Then, when she got to know Ralph, or Ghassan, or Husn, she stopped going to him. She decided to end her story with Abu Abd, and with that silent staircase, where she'd seen herself lonely in Beirut's long nights. There was a bit of pain and ecstasy exploding within her as she staggered between a feeling of disgust with her body and that feeling of fire sprouting in her eyes. But Husn was different, strange.

Alice told Gandhi she didn't understand men.

Gandhi was walking alone, with sadness all around him, when he met Alice just as she was about to enter the nightclub.

She told him she didn't understand men.

He was trying to tell her how disappointed he was with his son. Why wouldn't he marry Rima and end his relationship with Nuha Aoun?

Alice was trying to talk to him about men. And Gandhi knew too well. When he worked at Salim Abu Ayoun's restaurant in Beirut, he realized that life was full of secrets. The owner of the restaurant had died and left all the work to his wife. Najat, or Um Hasan, ran everything. It was a small restaurant at the end of Abu Talib Lane. It was there that Gandhi discovered the secret. This was what he told his wife the morning after they were married. He told her women were different. But his wife didn't complain as Um Hasan always did. Gandhi did everything in the restaurant. He fried potatoes and eggplant, washed dishes, peeled onions and garlic, and slept there. He agreed to work for her because she gave him a place to sleep in a little attic above the restaurant. But he discovered that she only wanted him to sleep there in order to keep an eye on the place. Every night after he finished working, she'd prepare a special meal, take a bottle of arak, climb up to the attic, and tell Gandhi to stay downstairs.

"If anyone comes, tell them there's no one here, we're closed. Got it?"

"Got it, Ma'am," Gandhi would say, looking down at the floor, because he was too shy to look that woman in the eye.

Then Mr. Spiro would come. Gandhi called him Spiro with the hat, because he never took off his blue beret, in order not to show his bald head. Mr. Spiro would come, go up to the attic, and downstairs Gandhi would sit, glued to his chair, listening to their sighs and moans.

Um Hasan would ask him to do the mopping when Spiro came. Gandhi would roll up the bottoms of his pants, put the chairs up on the tables, and mop. Then, when the sounds would start, he'd feel as though his back would break in two. He'd lean up against the wall and listen, imagining the scene as he pleased, Um Hasan's large breasts between Mr. Spiro's hands, Spiro's bald head under her breasts, twinkling with sweat. And he'd remember his father's Gypsy wife and the sting of his stick against his face, back, and thighs. He'd lean against the wall holding the world between his hands and groaning loudly. But Um

Hasan wouldn't hear him, and Spiro was nonexistent, high in ecstasy, deaf to everything.

Little Gandhi would go on mopping the floors as he watched Spiro leave. Then Um Hasan would come downstairs without looking at him. She'd glance aside as if she were saying good-bye. Then the darkness of the streets would swallow her up, leaving Gandhi all alone to wash the empty plates that had been piled beside his bed, and he'd sleep on the odor of Spiro's sweat, Um Hasan's perfume, his own sighs buried in the silence of drowsiness.

Little Gandhi was afraid of this man Spiro. He owned a bicycle rental shop and Gandhi didn't like bike riding. He'd heard that Spiro had some dubious relationships with the kids who rented bikes from his shop. And that day, when Little Gandhi was put in charge of cleaning the streets in the quarter, he saw Mr. Spiro, hardly able to walk, his grandson Nabil walking beside him.

The Reverend Amin said that Spiro almost collapsed when his son, a graduate of AUB and an employee in an advertising agency, refused to name his son Spiro after his grandfather.

"You want people to laugh at the boy?" his son asked.

"Laugh? Why should they laugh? Is Spiro such a horrible name?"

"No, Dad, not horrible, but it's not for a little boy."

"What, was I born old? Wasn't I a little boy once? I was, and my name was Spiro, and I was proud of my name."

"It's up to me to call him what I want."

"You're not my son, that's for sure. Your mother must've gotten you somewhere else. Is Spiro such a shameful name? It's after Saint Spirodonius the Miraculous. Your generation is full of shit."

Spiro warmed up to this grandson. He started teaching him prayers and would read him the "synaxarion." He'd bribe him with money and chocolate to get him to listen to the stories of Saint Spirodonius the Miraculous, whose saintliness was heralded by donkeys. They slaughtered the two donkeys in the middle of the night and ran away. Saint Spirodonius got up and put their heads, which were dripping with blood, back in their places. In the morning the people believed it was a miracle when they saw the white donkey's head on the black donkey's body and the black donkey's head on the white one's body. The boy would fall asleep next to his grandfather, and the grandfather would try to read from this ancient book, which he inherited from his grandmother Hanna. He'd put on his spectacles over his large black nose and read the stories of "Ireni."

"His daughter's name was Ireni, and he made her speak after she was dead."

The grandson seemed doubtful and Spiro would read alone, hearing his own voice as it metamorphosed into a voice resembling his grandmother Hanna's. The same intonation, the same "ahems," the same grandson, but this one's name was Nabil, not Spiro. And Spirodonius the Miraculous would be ticked off and would no longer be interested in forgiving the sins of this blasphemous family.

Spiro walked, leaning on the cane in his right hand, with his grandson Nabil walking beside him. He'd walk up and down Hamra Street mumbling in a muffled voice, his grandson unable to hear him. He stood in front of Little Gandhi and spoke with him. The war had wiped out the differences between people, and Spiro with the hat increased his visits and conversations with Little Gandhi. And he didn't stop visiting him until after they discovered the body of Madame Nuha Aoun the night of September

15, 1980. When it happened, the Assyrian storekeeper Habib Malku said, "They're murderers and we can't do anything about it." But Malku didn't agree that the situation had anything to do with sectarianism or the feast of the cross. Malku was the one whose grandfather fled from Marsin in 1918 by foot during the massacres in Turkey. He still remembered his grandfather with his swollen feet, speaking in Turkish, his head wrapped in a black cloth. He remembered how he'd sleep sitting up in the bamboo chair.

Malku, unlike his grandfather, never stopped talking. He was the most popular guy in the quarter. He'd roll his *r*'s and swallow up half of his *l*'s as he bragged, saying, "We're the real Arabs. Al-Akhtal[8] was Assyrian. He used to enter upon the Umayad Caliph with wine dripping from his beard . . . the greatest Arab poet was from the tribe of Taghlib, and the tribe of Taghlib was Assyrian."

The Reverend Amin, who avidly studied the Ghassanid roots of the Greek Orthodox sect, to which he no longer belonged thanks to his father the cobbler who'd become a Protestant at the hands of the American missionaries, used to make fun of Malku and the way he talked. "The members of the tribe of Taghlib were Arabs, and this guy's Assyrian. What do you mean, did al-Akhtal recite his poetry in Arabic or Syriac? What, is Syriac Arabic? The world's gone mad. We are the Arabs. We fled when the Marab Dam collapsed and we came to Huran, and we made a kingdom and allied ourselves with the Muslims. But look at this end we've reached. The kingdom has become a dump. Hamra Street has become a dump, and the Assyrian has become the descendent of al-Akhtal!"

---

8. Al-Akhtal is one of the three famous Umayyad poets who professed his Christianity openly and entered the caliph's palace wearing a big cross.

Gandhi liked Habib Malku, but he didn't know how to befriend him. This man, who was one of the best watch repairmen in Beirut, and owned a store in Bab Idriss, wound up buying that store near his house after he lost his eyesight. He turned it into a shop that sold everything from fresh produce to notebooks. The back of the store was filled with old utensils and small kerosene stoves. It became his hobby to collect these antique kerosene stoves that people no longer used and carefully line them up on the shelves in the back of the store.

The night before he died, Gandhi stood for a long time in front of the store, where the old Assyrian was rubbing his hands together and saying, "The war is over. Damn the Jews, but now the Jews are here—who'd have said the Israeli army would reach Beirut. What do we care. Jews? Fine. The important thing is it's all over."

Gandhi left the store because he didn't know what to say. He left the store and walked alone on his final journey, where he met Alice at the Montana. That day Alice didn't talk much. No one knew what she would've said. She was worried about the owner of the Salonica Hotel—that white Egyptian who couldn't find anywhere except downtown, which was on the verge of destruction, to buy a building and turn it into a hotel. And Alice, who understood the male psyche, figured it out in a flash, from the outset, that this man was running a whorehouse and trafficking hashish. But with the deterioration of things, the hotel became something of a shelter house, a place to sleep for what was left of the Egyptian barmaids, lots of soldiers, and herself. Alice used to say these soldiers are nothing like the soldiers she used to know. She was worried the Israeli soldiers would do something to the hotel owner, and she told the story of Lieutenant Tannous.

"What a catch he was. Gorgeous, and so slim he could slide his body through a wedding ring. Handsome, tall, and elegant; spiffy and à la mode. But what a loss; he turned out to be a sissy. Once they're in the presence of women, men become women. I understand men," she said to Gandhi. "In the presence of women men become women. He was a macho man around men, but with women, he was a wimp. And that's what your son's like with Madame Nuha."

Alice's story with Lieutenant Tannous was a long one. We don't know where it begins, but we do know where it ends, because Alice tells the end clearly. It's the beginning we don't understand well. Maybe it's because things got all mixed up in Alice's mind, or because she didn't want to tell us the truth. This obscure beginning starts with her escape from Shekka. Alice told us she was an only daughter. Her mother died and her father never remarried. He was a fisherman and was always drunk. Here Alice would tell the beginning in classical fashion, for the majority of the prostitutes in our country began their profession after being raped by their fathers. And this is precisely Alice's situation. She'd talk about a bad childhood, how she started working as a maid at age thirteen, and how she remembers nothing of her father except the way he smelled of fish, and how he used to hit her, and she remembers her loneliness. Back then Shekka was a small village, and the man who was called Abboud Murad spent his time between the sea and gambling. Alice said he raped her, but her memories concerning this subject were muddled, because when he came to her, drunk, in the middle of the night, she felt only a minor pain between her thighs. She felt him on top of her, but went on sleeping just the same. She didn't know why she didn't dare let him know she was awake. When he finished, he went back to his bed, which was on the floor next to hers, and she listened to him snore. Alice didn't leave the house right away after that. She was ten years old and believed the time to leave home would be when she got married. But after what had happened, and she understood what had happened, because she knew all about it, she decided to run away. Then a year later she got her chance. The man was a friend of her father's, a fisherman, forty-five years old, older than her own father. He told her he was going to Beirut and asked her to go with him. He said a relative of his had gotten him a job at the port, he had a place to stay, and he wanted to marry her. Alice knew the man was lying to her, but she ran away with him anyway. She lived with him in a small room on Wegand Street and there the whole world opened up for her. She stayed with the man three years. He didn't marry her, and she didn't ask him why. She knew when she ran away with him he wasn't going to marry her. And on Wegand Street she fell into the snares of Abu Jamil, and the world opened up before her. Alice was fourteen, and Beirut was just beginning. Beirut's nightlife began in the mid-forties, and from there Alice began her journey.

Even though this beginning sounded like the stories of other prostitutes, hers differed in that she never claimed she didn't like the profession. One of those nights in the Salonica Hotel, she herself said, after telling me the story of Lieutenant Tannous and drinking half a bottle of arak, which made her hands stop shaking, that she couldn't stand how some of her prostitute friends constantly came up with this nonsense about hating the profession. Alice said she enjoyed her life a lot, she loved and lived.

"If it hadn't been for the impresario Abu Jamil, I'd still be with that old man, in that dark room. I'd be a maid, working for nothing. With Abu Jamil things were different. He took me and made a lady out of me, and the world opened up for me. With him I discovered real pleasure, the pleasure to dance and drink and live. With him I learned about love. But my true love was Tannous, God love him. I don't know where he ended up, but I know one thing. He was a man, and it was I who told him to go."

Alice worked at Shaheen's nightclub, and it was there she met George, "king of the night." Abu Jamil warned her about him, said he kills women. But he was extraordinarily handsome, indescribably beautiful; thick blond hair, tall, fair, and rich. He'd sit down at a table and everyone would rush to his service. He'd wave his hand and the champagne bottles would be popped open. Money just poured from his pockets, and it was nothing to him. He saw Alice after she finished her dance routine. Alice wasn't a dancer, she was a cocktail waitress, but from time to time she'd dance when the owner Salim al-Hibri would ask her to do a short number. King of the night requested her, so she came. For the first time in her life, she was awestricken and got drunk. She sat and started drinking while he doled out his smiles and jokes to the crowd. Then he took her by the hand and went. She didn't change out of her dance clothes; she went with him half-naked. He took her to his apartment and there they kept the night fires burning till dawn; he sang and she danced until she passed out. He left her there on the living room floor and went to sleep in his bedroom. But before he went to sleep, he leaned over and kissed her and said he wanted to see her the next week at the Epi Club. When Alice got up the next morning, there was no one but herself in the apartment. She called Abu Jamil, and he brought her clothes and took her to his house. Two days later the white king died; someone had put a booby trap under his bed. There were rumors he was an Israeli spy. But Alice didn't believe the stories about the white king. Tannous told her night was starting to slip away, and when night slips away, day falls apart. Alice didn't understand at all. She was annoyed with Tannous because every time he slept with her, he'd start talking politics. He'd sit on the edge of the bed, light up a filterless Lucky Strike, talk, and cough. She worried about his health because of those damned cigarettes while he went on about politics and told her the secrets of the night. He said the problem with the white king was that he was selling the white stuff and it's hard to bust cocaine dealers because they operate in areas that are hard to control.

"We grow hashish; we know the story from A to Z. They smuggle it to Egypt and Israel. No problem, hashish is a national resource, and it's not bad for you. But cocaine, where does it come from? We don't know. This means it's slipped out of our hands. Night is running away, Alice. God help us."

Alice didn't understand how night could slip away. And what did this officer have to do with smuggling hashish, and why did they kill the white king? She was convinced he'd been working for the Israelis, as Abu Jamil told her, and she loved Abu Jamil. With his white hair, small eyes, and deep olive complexion, and his Adam's apple bobbing up and down, Abu Jamil inspired her with a strange confidence. This eccentric man, a Beiruti down to his bones, who lived only at night, treated his hookers as his own daughters.

"I'm a religious man," he'd say. "I don't take what isn't mine."

When Alice found out he was married and lived a traditional life in the Ramal al-Zarif area, and his wife wore a veil, she wasn't surprised. Alice saw Abu Jamil as the model of what a real man should be. He rarely drank. He'd put his drink down in front of him, and the glass would get more full as the ice melted, and he himself would constantly add more ice. Abu Jamil told her that the king of the night was a spy and that the Armenian Kasparian was the one who organized the network that was set up to catch Arab military attachés and question them for Israel, and he used to murder young women using a syringe he got from a Turkish doctor who belonged to the organization. When things were exposed, Kasparian got out of it, sold the Epi Club, and took off to Brazil. Lieutenant Tannous said nice guys always finish last; Kasparian got away and the white king died.

Tannous would tell how the white king's story was extremely complicated. This young White Russian orphan, who was called George Ivanhoe, was picked up by Shahnaz the Turkish dancer, who turned him into her servant. And like magic he became one of the kings of Beirut's nightlife. No one knew how it happened. He took over Kasparian's business and things just took off for him. Then when the game was uncovered, he became the victim. Alice remembers her night with him; she remembers how handsome he was, how kind, how he reminded her of teardrops.

"He was something else, like teardrops in your eyes."

Tannous was inflamed with jealousy.

"You love me only out of jealousy. You don't really love me, you love being jealous. That's how it is with all men."

But Tannous was serious. He rented a house, furnished it, then took Alice to it and said to her, "This is your house."

Alice refused to quit her job.

"Leave everything and I'm yours."

She wouldn't do it. "I wouldn't," she said, "because I knew he'd leave me. Men have always left me, and I've always been alone." She looked around and laughed.

"See what I mean. Aren't I alone now? I have no one except God." She pointed up with her finger.

Tannous didn't leave Alice so easily. He lived with her for three years. He used to wait for her everyday in front of the club and walk her home. He'd never stop smelling her all over. He'd tell her the smell of her body drove him wild, that he loved her body. She was very much in love. She understood that something that takes you nowhere and leaves you lost. Alice remained lost for three years. It's true she never stopped working, but she could feel his eyes staring at her wherever she was. This young lieutenant's eyes haunted her.

"I'll give you the world."

She loved him. She didn't want the world; she wanted him. She loved him, and loved his children and his wife. He never talked to her about his wife. But she saw her once with him and his two children. They were at the amusement park. He'd mentioned to her they were going there that Sunday afternoon, and so she went. She didn't put on any makeup, or high heels. She wore a simple dress and put her hair in a ponytail and went. She sat alone on the bench waiting. Then she saw them. She wanted to hop off the bench and hug the children. But she didn't move. He was playing and eating popcorn with the children, and every now and then he'd catch a glimpse of her out of the corner of his eye. Then she walked toward them. They were standing in front of the Pepsi vendor. As she got closer, she could see the fear in Tannous's eyes, as though he'd seen the devil himself. She saw how his face twitched and the muscles contracted. She bought a Pepsi and left.

When he came to see her the next day, he was horrified. She said she loved the children and that his wife was beautiful, and that she cared for everything he cared for.

After that experience at the amusement park, he changed and became less talkative. Alice fell more in love. That's when she realized that love is jealousy.

"Love doesn't exist if you don't get jealous, if you don't feel that the other person is not really yours."

This is what she used to say when she'd try to make excuses for the way Husn behaved around Madame Nuha.

"You see, my dear Gandhi, Husn is in love, in other words totally lost. He can't stand to be without the woman for one minute, and that explains everything."

"God help him," Gandhi said and went to work. Gandhi didn't have any more work to do. Being in charge of keeping the streets clean became pointless. With the deterioration of things as a result of the situation in Beirut in 1980 and 1981, explosives were all over the place. People became afraid of garbage collection areas because these had become the perfect place to plant bombs. So Gandhi was content with merely picking up the black trash bags from people's houses and throwing them in the dump near Khayyam Cinema. As for driving the garbage truck around, he gave that up altogether, and with time he also stopped picking up people's trash and taking it to the dump. The first of every month he'd make his rounds and take his pay, as if he'd become a beggar. And that's how he felt; or as if he were blackmailing people. But it had become impossible for him to go back to his old line of work, and he didn't decide to go back to it until the morning of September 15, 1982, when the Israelis entered Beirut and the city was filled with their black boots, their beards, and their stench. This was the day Gandhi would die, on top of his shoe-shine box, and the story would end. And when all trace of Alice would be lost, in 1984, after the war broke out anew in the city, we would lose track of all the characters in this novel. Even traces of the Reverend Amin, tucked away in the nursing home in Ashrafiyyeh, would be lost.

When Alice lost touch with Lieutenant Tannous, she became very depressed and would cry all the time. She'd be in the bar sitting with the customers until four in the morning, drinking with them. She'd let them get close to her and kiss her and she'd listen to their stories, and there she'd cry every night, with every story she heard. It got to the point where the owner wanted to fire her, but the impresario Abu Jamil saved her by sending her to Mosul. There Alice discovered a different kind of love and began to forget.

"The best part about love is forgetting it. Being able to forget is what makes us human." That's what she'd say while she told the story of "The Leader."

Alice was tired of her work, of Beirut, of Tannous, and of her tears. The revolution of 1958 brought about a frightening increase in business, especially after the arrival of the marines, who would stay up all night carousing. Then the marines disappeared after the whorehouse incident when Abu Mansour kidnapped one of them while he was with the prostitute Samia the Copt, and didn't release him until the president of the republic himself stepped in and after he got an unknown sum of money.

And she left.

This time she didn't work in the nightclub as she had agreed with Abu Jamil. She went directly to Baghdad Hotel, and she was not allowed to leave the hotel or talk to anyone. At night the same man would come and take her to the black room, and the story that took place two years earlier repeated itself. But this time Alice had to sleep on the side of the bed next to the table, because that's what he'd made her do the first night. She felt as though his left hand were tied to his neck, but she didn't say anything. She went where he told her to go. He kissed her shoulder and lay down on his back, motionless. She spent the whole night waiting for him to move. Even his breathing was slight. And his old smell, the smell of dusty clothes and salt, faded away. Alice started going to that black room to sleep, and after two weeks she decided to go back. She couldn't take the boredom, they killed her, boredom and this dark corpse that would get dressed and sleep next to her. But she didn't dare talk about it. A whole month went by. Alice didn't know where she got the courage. The man was lying on his back as if he were dead and she sat up and said she was going to leave the next day. No response. She said she was bored with spending the whole day in the hotel with nothing to do except crossword puzzles. No response. She said she missed dancing and asked him if he wanted her to dance for him. No response.

Alice got scared. She was afraid the man was dead. From the beginning she hadn't violated the rituals of that black room. She'd stay firm in her place on the bed and he was the one who'd come close and move away. But he stopped coming close. He'd enter the room, she'd notice a shadow entering, he'd throw himself down next to her and go to sleep. He even stopped kissing her. Alice wanted to know if his eyes were open or shut. She spent three days sleepless over this question. She went up close to him, but this time he didn't move or push her away with his right hand as he usually did. She went up close to him and kissed him. He was cold and tasted like a dead fish. Alice put her hand on his waist and he pulled back a little. Alice didn't know what came over her. A kind of anger inflamed her entire body when she saw him pull back, and she shouted.

"What do you want from me! Who the hell are you?"

She heard snoring, or something that resembled snoring, and she got the feeling the man was trying to stand up. She grabbed onto him, by his shirt, and his shirt almost tore in her hands. She went closer and laid on top of him and began kissing him. It was as though something were raging inside her. The man stayed still like a dead fish. Alice doesn't remember what happened exactly. She went down. She left his side and moved down to the bottom of the bed. She grabbed him by the balls and started to pull. When she grabbed him she didn't intend anything, but he didn't move, he just stayed there, totally still, his breathing increasing only slightly. Alice pulled harder and screamed, and amidst her hysterical screaming she heard him screaming, too, as if he were yelping like a dog. He pushed her and stood up.

"You, you!" she shouted.

"Hush, hush," the man sighed as he stood there.

"You are 'The Leader.' I know you, you son of a bitch."

He ran around the room and then he disappeared.

Alice ran away. She said no one objected to her leaving. The next day she went to the airport and returned to Beirut.

Lieutenant Tannous didn't run away. It seemed his wife found out. On one of those mornings while Tannous was shaving before leaving for his house, with Alice standing by his side in the bathroom, watching the shaving cream on his face and the razor sliding and turning his face into a mirror, the doorbell rang. Alice put her robe on over the nightgown she was wearing and opened the door. She was shocked. She couldn't open her mouth.

"Are you Alice?" the woman asked.

"Yes. Come on in."

Alice's body trembled slightly.

"Where's Tannous?"

"Please come in, Ma'am."

The woman came in. Tannous's wife had blond hair, long eyelashes, a full figure, and skin as white as snow.

"Tell him I want to see him."

"Make yourself at home."

The woman sat on the edge of the sofa and Alice sat in front of her, not knowing what to do.

"Would you like a cup of coffee?"

"I told you I want him. Where is he?"

Alice left her there in the middle of the room and rushed to the bathroom to find Tannous naked in front of the mirror, totally confused. All of a sudden Alice noticed his paunch, which was getting bigger, and the hair on his back, which was like an ape's. She told him; she tried to tell him. He motioned to her as if he wanted to stop her voice from coming out. He got dressed in a hurry and went to the living room. Alice hesitated before following behind him, and then she saw him as he really was.

Alice said it was the first time she really saw him. Before then she hadn't seen him for what he was. And now there he was, standing there, his wife standing there next to him. Alice leaned over the side entrance to the living room, alongside the dining room, and didn't say a word.

His wife asked him for a divorce.

"Divorce me, Tannous. Divorce me and marry this whore, I don't care, but let me go. They told me, but I wouldn't believe it. George's wife told me, but I didn't believe her. She told me, Your husband is having an affair and you think he's out working all night. You're an idiot. She told me I was an idiot. And you'd come home early in the morning tired and dead. I'm the dead one now."

She started screaming and threw herself onto the floor, trembling. Alice thought she might have passed out, so she ran to the kitchen and brought some orange blossom water and sugar and kneeled over her.

"Get up. God help you."

The woman pushed the flower water away and stood up.

"Come with me, you son of a bitch, I'll tell everyone about you."

At this point something strange happened. Alice was expecting Tannous to yell at her or hit her, but instead he bowed his head to her and went home.

And whenever Alice would remember him after that, she'd think of a white puppy dog with his tail between his legs. Maybe it was because she'd told the story so many times and she'd always end it by saying, "He put his tail between his legs and followed her home." Or maybe it was because of his white pants and white shirt, everything about him was white when he left. Like a white puppy dog with his tail between his legs.

He disappeared for a whole week. Then he came back and told Alice he loved her, but he couldn't live with her anymore.

She told him it was over, that she'd packed up his things in a suitcase and would leave the house at the end of the month and she'd rented a small apartment in Ayn Mraysi.

When she said good-bye to him she didn't feel anything. Even when he insisted on making love to her and she accepted, she didn't feel anything. Then came the sorrow. She was struck with a grief so terrible she couldn't talk about anything anymore. At one point she considered committing suicide and almost did with a leather belt she bought for Tannous's thirty-third birthday but never gave him.

He had told her, It's only three months until I turn thirty-three and die, just like Jesus Christ.

At the time, Alice laughed at him and his illusion and she went out and bought him the belt. But he left before his birthday came.

Alice was frightened by the religious spells that overcame that man. Often after sleeping with her he'd start praying in Syriac. He'd chant an entire Maronite liturgy naked and then he'd begin his political speech.

She took the belt and decided to hang it from the ceiling and kill herself. She got a chair, stood on it, and tried to tie the belt to the metal ring attached to the ceiling for the light bulb. She tied it to the ring and came down. She burst into tears and climbed onto the chair, but instead of hanging herself she untied the belt. She got down and ran to the porch and threw it. Then she burst into a mixture of laughter and tears.

When Gandhi listened to these stories he felt stupid, because he had no stories like these of his own to tell. He lived a life of safety and stability. His few adventures into the whorehouse passed without much excitement; watching the television, the woman watching and refusing to take off her bra and telling him to hurry up—none of these was stories worth telling.

On the other hand, the story of his daughter was entirely different, and the suffering she caused him while he took her from sheikh to sheikh. This was a story that made him sad and quiet. And Husn didn't care about anything except Madame Nuha. But why? Was it because he was jealous, or because he really loved her, or because she gave him money? Husn never told anyone the real story about that woman. Actually, he told Rima a little bit of it. He told her about his feeling of superiority with her, of feeling like a complete man.

Husn didn't tell the truth and the truth cannot be told. That's what he believed, because when it is told it becomes like a lie, and then it loses its importance. Instead the story itself becomes the issue.

Husn's problem, or Ralph's, as Madame Nuha Aoun used to call him, was simple. For Ralph, whose father sent him to the Evangelical School in Beirut, through the good offices of the Reverend Amin and Dr. Atef Nazzal and others, declared himself useless.

"Your son is a lost cause, Mr. Gandhi," the principal, Mr. Nabih Khouri, told him. "He's a lost cause, he's failing everything. His mind is not on his studies. You should find him some trade to learn and let him work."

Gandhi had wanted Husn to become a doctor, like Atef Nazzal, who had become a good friend of Gandhi's. Through Atef, Gandhi discovered that doctors were regular people like everyone else. Husn should become a doctor, but he was hardheaded and didn't study. He spent his time watching TV and playing pinball.

After long discussions, lots of effort, and lots of patience, Gandhi finally gave in to his son's plan. He said he'd found a job. Husn was nineteen years old, of medium height but on the short side, had black hair that was kept meticulously neat, and small eyes. He didn't look anything like his father except for his dark olive complexion and the way he stuttered when he spoke.

Husn decided to leave school because he hated the atmosphere of being under house arrest, and because he was a "lost cause," as the principal had told his father. He got himself a job in Ahmad's Hair Salon on Madame Curie Street in Beirut. The work fascinated Husn. It was in the salon that he changed his name to Ralph, and it was there he discovered the world of perfumes.

He'd come early in the morning, mop the salon with this fragrant soap. He'd pour out the liquid soap, which had a yellowish color to it, and mop the floors. Then he'd rearrange the chairs and wipe them with a brown cloth and wait. He was crazy about women's hair. When he'd watch the strands falling through Master Ahmad's fingers, he felt he was watching a real magician. He'd breathe in the smell of the dyes and spray and perfume. Ralph's relationship with the salon was his entrance into the world of women. There he saw women; women quite different from the wives of the refugees who were forced out of their villages in the south and were living on Hamra Street. They were fashionable, sexy, speaking in Arabic and French and with them Ahmad the hairdresser was a magician. After having their hair shampooed by Rafiq, Ahmad's assistant, they would flirt with him and wait without getting bored as they told their stories and jokes, laughing and giggling before Ahmad's wandering glimmering eyes. Magazines and pictures and women and Ralph would watch while nobody paid any attention to what he was doing. After a while, Ralph began to learn how to shampoo hair, and here the real ecstasy began. His fingers would slide through their hair and the women would melt in his hands, heads laid back on the metal basin. They'd surrender to their flowing hair while the smell of apples emanated from his hands. Actually this smell was a mixture of apple and other perfumes that reminded one of jasmine; it intoxicated Ralph. His hands would dive into their hair, into their closed eyes, as Ralph worked in a state of semiconsciousness. The smell made him dizzy and the feel of hair sent chills running up and down his spine. Then the women would get up with their wet hair, sit under the dryer, and start talking. Ahmad would cut and style, and when he was all done he'd give them what looked like a metal sash to wear before spraying their hair.

The first time Ralph used hairspray on Madame Nuha Aoun's hair he felt as though he were flying. As the spray streamed over her hair Ralph fluttered around her like a butterfly. Master Ahmad was quite pleased with this new assistant, for most of the professional ones had left. Joséf, the original owner, left, gave the keys to Ahmad, and just took off.

"That Joséf was something else," Madame Nuha would say. Joséf was great; it was impossible to get an appointment with him. But now after he left for some unknown place, along with all the rest of Lebanon's rising stars, it wasn't much fun anymore to go to the hairdresser.

Actually, Joséf was a woman, prettier than a woman. That's how all the women who came to his salon felt about him. He was known for his intimacy and elegance. He talked like women, with a penchant for detail, and laughed out loud like women. He had long tapering fingers, a long white face tinged with red, a long delicate nose, long eyelashes, thin eyebrows, and a soft voice that crackled with laughter whether or not there was reason to laugh. Joséf took off. He left Beirut, said he was going to Rome, and never came back. Master Ahmad, his first assistant, who took over managing the salon, said he was living in Jounieh.

"He left the business and went into buying and selling land."

The last day he was in West Beirut he was scared to death. He embraced Ahmad and said to him, "My sweetheart, the place is yours. Take care of things; I'll be back." Ahmad tried to persuade him to stay and told him he'd ransom him with his own eyes. But Joséf was even scared of Ahmad.

"I'm afraid of you, darling. Maybe you'll kill me; how do I know?"

"How could you say that? You taught me everything I know."

"This is true, but I'm leaving."

Joséf embraced Ahmad and started to cry. He walked away and never came back.

Ahmad had never thought about killing his teacher Joséf. It was true that after it became commonplace for shops to be bombed, he told his wife he was afraid and was thinking about taking down the sign from in front of the salon. Then he cursed Joséf and all Christians, and said that the salon was his, that he'd been working in it for thirty years and barely made enough to feed his family. But deep down he never thought about killing Joséf or taking over his shop. Joséf had taught him all he knew about the trade, and through him he met the most beautiful women in the world. From Sabah to Farah Diba to Afghani princesses. He lived like a king with him.

"Joséf was a king," Ahmad told Ralph. "He dished out money and the money kept on coming. But kings always end up being the butt of jokes in the end. I didn't let that happen to him. May God protect him."

Ralph knew that Madame Nuha would never love him the way she loved Joséf. Ahmad told him all about how she was a different woman under Joséf's hands. She didn't read magazines like the others; she surrendered herself like a chicken. She appeared to be sighing or as if she were about to choke, and she'd come out looking as beautiful as the moon, her smile overtaking half of her face, and Joséf hovering around her like some kind of god.

"Those were the days, not like now. Now we style hair as if it were work. In those days it was an art, and women were real women."

Madame Nuha didn't pay any special attention to Ralph. Joséf's story with her and the way she moaned excited him and made him feel out of breath. When he'd see her coming in and imagined Joséf dancing around her hair, his breathing would become short and choppy. Then he'd forget, until she'd start. She was the one who started it all.

"You started it," he told her.

She laughed, lying there naked on her wide bed. She laughed and didn't respond.

"You make me laugh, boy. Come here."

He'd come and make passionate love to her. She'd take him in, into her insides. Ralph would shake violently inside this white woman. She had a blinding whiteness about her. Ralph would always ask her to turn off the light, but she always left it on.

"I like to see your face, how handsome it becomes. I like to see you."

It all began. Madame Nuha sank down with her hair under the water while Husn was pouring on the apple-scented shampoo and delving his fingers into her long blond hair. Her head rose up for a moment and she looked at him but didn't say anything. Then she lowered her head back down.

"The water," she said. "The water."

"Would you like me to make it cooler?"

"No, no. The water's really nice."

She shook her head a little and then slumped down into the chair and Ralph finished his work. After having her hair dried Madame Nuha moved over to sit under Ahmad's fingers. Ralph couldn't keep his eyes off of her. He smudged Madame Ismail's forehead with black hair color while he was dying it for her. Madame Ismail screamed and so Master Ahmad ran over and cleaned her forehead with cotton and cigarette ashes mixed with water. Ralph paid no attention. He stood behind Madame Ismail's chair exchanging glances with Madame Nuha, who wasn't paying any attention to him.

Two days later he bumped into her on the street.

Ralph was on his way out of work from the salon and she was walking slowly down the street. He said hello to her and walked beside her and then they went to her house. Nuha Aoun lived alone in an old house with high ceilings and a garden grown over with grass. The smell of wool seeped from the walls. Her only daughter was living in the States and would write to her telling her to leave Beirut and come live with her. Her husband, Mr. Najib Aoun, was a fabric merchant in the Souq Tawila. He died in 1976 of a heart attack, leaving her with a lot of money, a daughter, and some demolished shops in the business district of Beirut. Her daughter would write telling her mother to come to California, and her mother would answer saying she couldn't leave Beirut. Her only friend was a French woman who was married to a Lebanese from the Shaheen family, and who worked in the French Cultural Center in Beirut. The husband had been kidnapped at the beginning of the war and the French woman kept moving between East and West Beirut waiting for her husband's release. Then she left the country. Arlette lost hope and left, and Madame Nuha was left all alone. Madame Nuha knew all the neighbors in the quarter, but she felt incapable of adjusting to the new situation. She acted as if she were waiting for some unknown thing to happen. She wrote to her daughter saying she was waiting, that Beirut was a storehouse of memories, but she didn't tell her the truth, and her daughter, who was living with her husband and two sons in San Francisco, couldn't understand her mother. She wrote to her saying she didn't understand, and that she'd given up on her.

Ralph didn't understand either.

She told him she was waiting for something, and that she would go. "What about me?" he asked her.

She almost died laughing. "You, sweetheart," she said, dragging out her words sarcastically.

"You, my son, see what the future holds for you. What do you want with me? I'm old enough to be your mother."

He hugged her close to him and smiled. He smiled like someone who pretends he understands but really doesn't.

Ralph was incapable of thought. This woman had taken him to the unknown. He slept with her every day, and felt as though she were drinking him and slurping him up. He'd go to her at eight o'clock at night, and they'd have dinner and then go to bed. The relationship was pure madness. She was a crazy woman. Her screams and moans engulfed Ralph's body and senses while he was around her and under her and on top of her as if he were lost.

"I can forget everything," he said to Rima after the story of Madame Nuha was over. He told her he could forget everything, but he didn't forget that one night. The rain poured over the windows, and Madame Nuha was waiting for him. He said he didn't know what happened to him, but he was like a child in her hands. She was the one who would take him and scream as he made love to her, but things would get away from him. She was everything, and he didn't remember, she would rise and fall and pull him back and forth and move away.

That night she cried, Ralph said. Pain was everywhere. My joints ached. And she, she became more beautiful, no one was more beautiful. Beautiful and glimmering under the lights. She put on her pink robe and walked around the house barefoot and started to sing. I stayed on the edge of the bed alone. I could feel her, but she wasn't herself.

Ralph said Nuha was not Nuha.

"How could a woman be another woman?" Rima asked.

"I don't know," Ralph answered. "I swear I don't know anything. I mean, I was there and she was there, but I wasn't really there. Until now her voice rings in my ears. I hear it but I don't understand. I feel like my body isn't my body."

"And with me, you don't feel?" Rima asked.

"No, it's different. You I love. With her it was pure lust. She controlled me. Not you, making love with you is like making love."

Rima thought about the concierge, but she didn't say anything.

And Husn didn't say anything. He didn't tell his father he killed the woman, Gandhi figured it out himself. He saw the smell of murder in his son's eyes. It was the same smell he saw for the first time in the eyes of Zaylaa, who later turned into a lamb in the Montana. Gandhi thought he could fix the matter with the help of Doctor Atef, since Doctor Atef had important friends in high places and could save Husn from the gallows. But no one investigated the murder of Madame Nuha. An officer from the Hbaysh precinct came by and filed a report and the corpse was taken to American University Hospital. The crime was considered a casualty of the war. No one knew how or where Madame Nuha was buried. Some said they couldn't find a grave for her and so they temporarily buried her in Mar Elias Btina Cemetery. Some said they couldn't find a Maronite priest to pray for her, and so a Protestant minister temporarily prayed for her. This was the exact opposite of what happened to the White Russian woman Vitsky Novikova, who died as a maid and was buried as a queen.

Madame Sabbagha went half-crazy. She called the bishop of Beirut and stood in front of her house wailing. Everybody came, all the families of Ras Beirut attended the funeral of Vitsky Novikova. Heading the procession was the bishop of Beirut, the Reverend Amin, the leaders of the political parties, even the Soviet ambassador was planning to attend but couldn't make it. The coffin was carried out of Mar Elias Church surrounded by women in black, incense burners, icons, and wreaths. Madame Sabbagha stood in front waving a black handkerchief; next to her was her stupid daughter who didn't know how to talk. From then on people said Madame Sabbagha had gone crazy. She started following the Reverend Amin in the streets, ranting and raving about this and that scandal, until finally one of her relatives came along and took her and her daughter away. After that, no one heard anything about her.

Ralph didn't want to kill Madame Nuha. He didn't kill her. He told Rima she died, she slipped, hit her head on the bathtub, and died. Ralph said he carried her to her room because he thought she was still alive. Ralph was lying.

"You're a liar, Ghassan. You're a murderer, and I'm afraid of you," Rima said and left the house and never came back.

Ralph didn't want to. Madame Nuha told him. He came to her in the evening as usual. He was still intoxicated with what had happened the night before, which he told Rima all about, and which even now he didn't know how to tell. He came, ready as usual, to do all the things that made her laugh. Madame Nuha used to laugh a lot when Ralph stood up after making love with her and started imitating the Reverend Amin, his slow gait, the way he slurred every word that came out of his mouth, especially "You are the salt of the earth," which was almost impossible to understand. He came only to find Nuha telling him, "It's over".

"What's over?"

"It's over, Ralph, my darling. I'm going to get married, we can't do it anymore. I'm getting married next week. Please go."

There was a new tone in her voice, as if she were about to cry.

"And what about me?"

"You? How do I know?"

"Who is he?"

"Constantine. Constantine Mikhbat, a well-known businessman, and my late husband's friend."

"And how old is he?"

"Fifty-six."

"Do you love him?"

"I love him and he loves me. It's over, Ralph. You have to understand."

They were sitting in the living room, in the same place they were drinking whiskey and eating a light supper before going to bed.

She told him Constantine had always been in love with her and she had always turned him away. She couldn't understand how he, her husband's friend, could dare to talk to her about his love for her.

"But I was faithful. I never went out with him once. I let him hold my hand a few times, but never let it go beyond that."

"Then what happened?"

"My husband died in the war, and he started calling me every day. We'd meet once a week. I'd go to his house in Ashrafiyyeh because he was afraid to come here."

"And do you love him?"

"I told you I love him. It's not a game."

"Have you been sleeping with him?"

"What kind of question is this? Of course."

"You're sleeping with him and with me at the same time?"

"It's different with you. Him I want to marry. You're something else."

"You're a whore; come over here."

Nuha didn't move. Ralph was being careful not to look at her. The entire conversation had taken place without him looking at her. Nuha hadn't told Constantine anything about her relationship with Ralph, but she had intentionally wanted to sleep with Ralph before going to see Constantine. She didn't sleep with Ralph every night, as Ralph had told Rima, or as he had remembered. She refused him many nights, but the night before she was to go see Constantine Mikhbat in Ashrafiyyeh she made a point of sleeping with Ralph. She'd wake up the next morning radiant and beautiful, smelling like soap.

Ralph didn't know where the night had gone. They were in the living room and it was getting close to one o'clock in the morning. Madame Nuha was yawning. He moved over next to her and held her hand.

"No, Ralph. No more."

"What do you mean, no more?"

"It's over, I told you. We're over. You have to go home now. Get up. Come give me a kiss. Good night."

He went close to her and she kissed him on the cheek. He tried to hold on to her but she pushed him back. He fell onto the couch, sitting down. He tried to stand up and almost fell.

"You're tired. Shall I make you a cup of herbal tea?"

"No. I don't want anything." He tried to get up. He stood up and the whole world started to spin.

She told him he could sleep there. "It's all right. You can sleep here if you want."

She went and got some sheets and a blanket for the sofa in the living room. Ralph took off all his clothes and threw himself naked onto the couch and covered himself with a green wool blanket.

She sat next to him and kissed his forehead.

"You know I love you," she said.

"And I love you."

He grabbed her by the hand and tried to pull her toward him.

She said no and went to her room, her three cats following behind.

One week later the smell started to seep from the house, and people found out that Madame Nuha Aoun had died of a sharp blow to the head, which caused internal bleeding and eventually led to her death. No one came to her burial. Even Mr. Constantine didn't come. He was in Greek Orthodox Hospital with an inflamed liver, which would eventually lead to his death, in his own bed, all alone.

Rima was listening to Ghassan's story and trying to get closer to him, but he kept moving farther away. His distance was comforting to her in a strange way.

"There's comfort in betrayal," she said to him once. "You're unfaithful to me and I feel I'm free. Freedom is betrayal."

He would look at her as if she were far away. He could never get close to Rima. He'd go out with her and spend the night out with lots of different friends, but he never once felt that kind of overwhelming love he felt with Nuha. He didn't know how he lost touch with Nuha's scent in the days that followed, but he became distant. At the salon he could hardly work, and Master Ahmad started looking at him differently, as though he were afraid of him.

Alice told Gandhi that Husn's story wasn't shocking.

"Men are like that. He'll forget everything. The best thing about us is that we are capable of forgetting. This is human nature. The important thing is to take care of your daughter."

How could he take care of his daughter, when he knew nobody wanted her? His wife, Fawziyya, was silent about the matter. She never talked about anything, that's how she always was, from the day they got married. When Gandhi would come home, she'd come in, quiet, always yawning, not say a word. He'd discuss their daughter's situation, but she wouldn't respond or seem to care. Nothing moved her, nothing, as if she were unconscious. Even the dog she made no objection to. When it was brought to their house in Nabaa, all she said was "It's filthy" and spit. But she put up with it. Gandhi knew that every time the dog came into the house she'd mop up after it, but she never protested. And when Gandhi killed the dog, following the advice of the Reverend Amin, she bathed and told her children and husband to bathe, as if the deceased were one of the family.

She said she was cleansing herself of the impurity. "God protect me from the dog and its filth."

Her relationship with their daughter frightened Gandhi. She wouldn't talk to her or feed her, as if she wanted to kill her. If Gandhi hadn't stuffed his daughter like a chicken every night she would've died of starvation.

Gandhi didn't know what he should do. Days became black. They'd taken Madame Sabbagha, the Reverend Amin had been smitten with senility and Alice took him to the nursing home, and Alice was different, and bombs were everywhere. The smell of the city became like the smell of dogs. Stray dogs filled the city streets and their barking increased night after night, as though they were standing right below the windows, barking. And the people walked, not hearing anyone or liking anyone. "Nothing. This is the city of nothingness." That's what Dr. Atef said when he ran into him that morning. Dr. Atef had changed a lot. He said he was suffering from toothaches and that his doctor, Dr. Gidigian, advised him to have them removed and replace them with dentures. He opened his mouth and Gandhi saw a mouth that looked like an abandoned cave.

"Oh my God, Doctor."

"What can we do, my son? This is old age. What's left of my life is less than what I've already used up."

"But the dentures don't look good. I've heard about implants. Why don't you have new teeth implanted and look like a young man again," Gandhi said.

"A young man, hah. You think this'll make us live forever? We'll finish removing the teeth and before we put in the dentures, we will have gone."

"Where to?"

"To there, on the road to no return."

"No big deal, Doctor."

"What do you mean, no big deal, my dear Gandhi? We're going to die and you tell me no big deal? It is a big deal. This is a university. You think of it as a university and a hospital. But, hey, what can I say to you? Mr. Gandhi, I swear shining shoes is better than what we do. A shoe shiner works with paint, and paint is color, and color is art. Your work is nicer than ours."

"But I quit and you're still a doctor. Tomorrow what do you say I'll pass by. This daughter of mine isn't getting any better."

"Tomorrow you'll go back to your work, don't worry. Do you think the situation is going to stay like this, with all these stupid committees and crap and tasteless war? We'll have a new government and you'll go back to your profession."

"And what about my daughter, Doctor?" Gandhi asked as he watched the doctor continue on his way.

"I told you go back to shoe shining. Take care of your shoe shining."

Dr. Atef left and Little Gandhi didn't see any more of him. They said he stopped going out of his house and no longer opened his door to anyone. His wife was having fainting spells but he refused to take her to the hospital. "God is the only healer," he'd say.

And Alice couldn't sleep anymore.

She had insomnia from the time she took up residence at the Salonica Hotel.

It's been a long journey, I told her.

So she asked me what journey I was talking about.

Nothing, I said. The book.

What book? she asked.

I didn't answer. She said she wanted some sleeping pills, but she was afraid she'd take them and die and they'd say she committed suicide, and suicide is a sin.

"Suicide is a sin, my son."

And Alice, who could no longer sleep, became a maid. She lost her job at the Blow Up after al-Askary's murder. Then she lost her apartment in Ayn Mraysi. Gandhi helped her get a job selling flowers at the Montana, but finding a suitable place for her to live was difficult. She slept at the Montana for two years, and there felt her joints would collapse from the humidity. Then she met the white Egyptian in the bar. He was looking for something. Even now Alice was not sure exactly what. She thought he was looking for prostitutes, that he wanted to set up his own network. He saw the possibility of using her as bait and so he suggested the hotel to her. She asked him why.

"I need you as an adviser, Madam. You can stay here for free. You're a gold mine."

So she started sleeping there. The war raged on, contrary to the Egyptian gentleman's predictions. The gold mine evaporated and the hotel turned into a meeting place for retired prostitutes and soldiers. Alice became a simple maid and nobody cared about her.

5

Alice said he died.

"I came and saw him, I covered him with newspapers, there was no one around, his wife disappeared, they all disappeared, and I was all alone."

Alice said she took him to the cemetery, and she saw the people without faces. "People have become faceless," she told me. She spoke to them and didn't get any response, then she left them and went on her way. That's how the story ended.

"Tell me about him," I said to her.

"How shall I tell you?" she answered. "I was living as though I were living with him without realizing it. When you live, you don't notice things. I didn't notice, I just don't know." She shook her head and repeated her sentence. "All I know is, he died, and he died for nothing."

I recall Alice's words and try to imagine what happened, but I keep finding holes in the story. All stories are full of holes. We no longer know how to tell stories, we don't know anything anymore. The story of Little Gandhi ended. The journey ended, and life ended.

That's how the story of Abd al-Karim Husn al-Ah-

madi al-Mughayiri, otherwise known as Little Gandhi, ended.

Death is black.

The newspapers covering the body of the little man dissolved under the light September rain. The color black oozed from the body, and the body swelled. The light rain poured down silently, and the newspapers got soaked and became transparent, the black words seeped out of them. The color black rolled onto the street to the curb filled with black trash bags.

Everything was black. Soldiers' boots, their rifles, their faces, their screams in the streets, and the hissing of bullets as they tore out buildings and windows.

Bullets, and silence. A dawn of light rain and boots, the city awakened as if it were asleep.

On Madhat Basha Street, a few meters from Saydani Street, Ahmad Sunbuk was running. On top of a garbage heap he found a wrinkled army uniform. He picked it up, put on the khaki pants over his own blue pants, and the army shirt over his own green one. He took off his brown shoes and put on the black rubber boots. Then he put a cooking pot on his head and went running in the streets.

Ahmad Sunbuk was looking right and left and laughing, baring his broken yellow teeth, and went running in the streets. He bent down, picked up a piece of wood, and put it under his arm like a machine gun. He aimed it at the street in front of him and started shooting. He started running and spraying bullets all around and making machine-gun sounds. He jumped over the trash bags and the little puddles that formed in the potholes in the road. He jumped up and fell on the ground, then got up again and continued his battle.

At the entrance to Saydani Street, Ahmad Sunbuk was hit with five bullets. The blood poured from his back, but he kept on running. Alice, who was standing over Little Gandhi's water-logged corpse, said he continued running as if he hadn't been hit. He was running, with the blood gushing from his back, and he didn't look back. His running began to slow down. He walked as he ran, then he fell to the ground as if he were acting. He fell on his knees and his head fell back and out came the cry "Allahu Akbar!"

It was Abu Saeed al-Munla who screamed. He came out onto the balcony and shouted "Allahu Akbar!" His voice was loud and hoarse, as if he were clearing his throat. And the cry "Allahu Akbar!" echoed from the minarets and balconies. Suddenly, the abandoned, demolished city began to shout from its minarets in a unified voice. The Israeli soldiers who occupied the streets, and who shot at anything and everything, aimed their rifles at Abu Saeed's balcony and fired. Abu Saeed was hit, the blood gushed from his chest like a fountain. He fell onto the floor of the balcony with a thud, and "Allahu Akbar!" sounded from all the minarets. The soldiers heard, fired, and then their rifles became silent. All of a sudden they began to retreat as if they were frightened. They bent down beneath the balconies, leaning their tired bodies against the walls, and kneeled with their knees to their chests on the ground. And Ahmad Sunbuk remained in his place, kneeling, his head thrown back as if he were praying.

Alice wept and wailed. She wasn't sure if she was crying over Gandhi or Sunbuk or Abu Saeed, or because she heard the calls of "Allahu Akbar!"

I asked her about Sunbuk. She smiled and wiped her eyes with a Kleenex, as though she wanted to show me she was about to cry. She said everyone knew Sunbuk, and no one knew who he was or where he came from. He was the local idiot. He'd stand in the middle of Hamra Street with a piece of gray cloth in his hand, using it to polish the windows of cars stopped in traffic. The people in the cars would get impatient with him, because when he'd wipe the glass he'd get it all dirty instead of cleaning it, leaving behind little black smudges. The drivers would pay him and accept his dirty piece of cloth to avoid upsetting him. Sunbuk wouldn't allow anyone to make fun of him. One time a man got out of his car, paid him, and asked him not to clean the windshield. The only thing Sunbuk could do was break the windshield of the car with one swift blow of his fist. Sunbuk changed after that incident. It was no longer enough for him to wipe windshields; now he'd stand up and whistle, direct traffic, and give orders.

Nobody knew anything about him other than that he came from a small village in the Beqaa. He never told anyone the name of the village, and he was all alone. He lived in a wooden shanty next to Ramal al-Zarif High School. He'd drink Pepsi out in front of his shack and sing in a soft voice.

What happened to Ahmad Sunbuk the morning of September 15, 1982? Was he a part of the river of blood the city was to drown in? Or was he its hidden cry amidst the fear that flattened the city's joints during three months of bombings and blockades?

Abu Saeed al-Munla said in the hospital while listening to the news of the massacres of Sabra and Shatila, and of the collective fear that overtook Beirut, he said something hidden inside him had made him scream. He didn't know why the call to prayer rose out of him, for it wasn't time for prayer.

On that morning, people said, the voices of the muezzins were different. In Beirut, as is the case in all the cities of this region, the muezzins no longer climbed up the minarets to sound the call to prayer. They replaced this with recordings connected to loudspeakers. As for that morning, things were different; they weren't recordings, they were the real voices of the muezzins, piercing the city sky. They were like wounds rising up in the middle of a silence that made it seem like gunfire, and faces like masks peered out from the windows. There was nothing left but the quick steps of the soldiers and the sound of their random firing, and the black fear drawn on the lines in their faces. The moans of the wounded dying in the streets of the abandoned city trailed off, with no one to hear their final cries for help.

This is how endings are. A rattling in the throat, voices calling out to come to prayer, and faint moaning covering the streets of an abandoned city.

Gandhi's mother didn't tell him she didn't hear his very first cries, because they came with the dawn prayers. The voice of Sheikh Khalil, the muezzin of Mashta Hasan, was echoing between the walls of the black clay houses. That's how Little Gandhi was born, after six sisters and prayers and solemn vows taken by his mother, Nafisa, the daughter of Haj Mahmoud al-Khayyat. Her prayers didn't do any good. Husn bin Abd al-Karim, Gandhi's father, married three other women under the pretense that his wife was infertile. The last of them was that Gypsy with the long black hair that led Gandhi to the cave of escape.

Nafisa had been married to Husn for seven years and hadn't gotten pregnant. After the first year he married a second wife, and two years after that a third. The night of Little Gandhi's birth he was contracting marriage with the Gypsy woman. But his wives gave him only girls. The day of the birth of his sole heir he was sleeping in a hut in a remote village with his Gypsy and no one dared to tell him. When he found out the next day and came to Nafisa, his eyes sparkling with happiness, he found she was unable to talk. She was flushed with fever from her head to her toes, delirious words dribbled out from her lower jaw. Her head was wrapped in a white cloth and Husn's wives were standing all around her. Husn took his son into his arms and said "Abd al-Karim, Abd al-Karim has come" and prayed over his head. Then he leaned over Nafisa and said something to her the other women didn't hear. He asked the midwife to rub kohl on the baby's eyes, then he returned him to his mother. Forty days later the mother died. People said that the Gypsy woman had cast a spell on her. The mother died and Abd al-Karim nursed from his father's second wife and lived among women and girls in a little village, in an ordinary family with nothing special about it except the image of this father who traveled a lot and beat up his wives.

Abd al-Karim didn't remember how he lost his left eye. He got used to living with only one eye, to seeing everything, without ever feeling that his left eye was blind. His aunt said his eye bled when he was forty days old. The mother died, and blood gushed from the baby's eye. His aunt took him to Sheikh Ibrahim, the village doctor who squeezed an herbal mixture into his eye, but it never got better. It became inflamed and covered with black spots. She took him to a bedouin who was known for treating incurable cases. He said the eye should be cauterized and so he heated a nail, cauterized it, and blinded it.

"I've spent my whole life with only my right eye. I see everything from the right. I'm used to that, and it's all right. I don't know why God created two eyes, it must be His wisdom, but as for me, it's all right this way."

That's what Little Gandhi said to Doctor Atef, many years after that incident, when he suggested Gandhi see an eye specialist at American University Hospital.

"Forget it, Doctor," Gandhi said and went on shining his shoes.

Gandhi didn't remember his childhood, for childhood in Mashta Hasan passed by as if it had never happened at all. He knew he was born around 1915, and that he went to the village Qur'an school, where he memorized the Holy Qur'an at the age of seven under the supervision of the blind teacher Sheikh Zakariyya Hamid. Then he went to the nuns' school for a couple years and then had to quit and stay at home when his father stopped paying his tuition. He didn't know why his father never took him to work with him. He used to leave him at home as if he were one of the girls. He remembered squatting for hours in front of his black house in Mashta Hasan. He remembered the great cliff that separated Mashta Hasan from Mashta Hammoud, and the green cornfields that stretched for miles.

Little Gandhi didn't eat at home. Most of the time his father's wives and daughters would send him out of the house. His father had only one son, and the house was full of wives and daughters. His father was always depressed and mean. He'd hit his wives and laugh out loud. Gandhi remembered those loud laughs that sliced through the thin curtain separating the room from the rest of the house. But he didn't remember his father's words.

Gandhi didn't remember much about the village he fled from, narrow roads, dirt, pebbles, freezing cold that made his teeth chatter. It was as though he never lived in that village, or as if he'd slept through it all. He'd mention how his greatest pleasure was to sleep. Their house consisted of a big room and a small room separated by a brown curtain. Everyone slept in the big room, which doubled as a living room for welcoming guests during the day. His father was the only one who would sleep on the brass bed in the small room with one of his wives.

Gandhi remembers sleep meant women. He'd sleep in a big room filled with women, with voices and arguments and shouting all around him. The floor of the big room was covered with mattresses, and on them slept the women with their daughters all around them, and he slept all alone in the southern corner of the room. He savored his aloneness. There Gandhi discovered pleasure, in the southern corner, all alone, and where he saw with one eye. Gandhi discovered the shadows of the women as they got undressed and laughed, and the smell of perfume that wafted out from their nightgowns.

Gandhi lived alone in the village. His father wasn't poor, but he didn't own any land; he sold it in order to get married. He owned a store in Arida, a village about a half-hour walk from Mashta Hasan. His father would go there every day riding on his donkey and come back in the evening with food.

Gandhi ate only at night, when his father returned. They'd sit alone in front of the tray of food placed on the floor and eat, the women coming and going around them without sitting down to eat. Gandhi would've preferred eating after his father finished, when the tray of food transformed into a party with the women and their daughters fighting over the pieces of bread and chick-peas planted on top of the cooked wheat. When Gandhi would sit with his father around the somber tray of food he had no desire to eat, for eating with his father was a sad, silent ritual, where all he heard was lips smacking over the food. But he was not allowed to eat with the women. The Gypsy woman his father married the moment of his birth would kick him out. He'd see the whites of her eyes as she motioned for him to go, and so he'd get scared and leave. He'd go to the courtyard near the door, squat down, listen, and take the leftovers of bread and food from one of his sisters, and then he'd go off on his daily excursion through the black dirt roads.

Gandhi had no recollection of his sisters; in his mind he pictured them all as one. When he returned to the village for his father's burial, he didn't recognize any of them. He embraced them and their husbands, but he didn't feel as though they were his sisters. Only the Gypsy woman was part of his memory of white eyes. He felt a special affection for her. With her worn out clothes and face covered with pimples, she reminded him of the beggars he met every day in the streets of Beirut. She asked him for money, so he gave it to her. She told him his aunt Khadija, who had nursed him as a baby, had been dead for two years, and that they sent for him to come, but he never came.

Gandhi was alone among them. He gave the Gypsy some money and decided to go back to Beirut. And in those fields that he did not recognize, he remembered only that smell. When he walked in the village at night, after the mourners left, nothing drew him to the place except that smell. Only the smell itself remained from his childhood, for childhood is a world of smells, and the world we leave behind we never go back to, because we don't know it. Gandhi knew nothing.

In the village he married his cousin.

His uncle sold lupine beans from a pushcart in the streets of Tripoli. He saw him at the wake but didn't recognize him. Poverty had devoured his eyes, and age had transformed him into the remnants of a man. The Husn Ahmad family, which traced back its roots to the sheikhs of the Akkar region, had lost all their property to time, fear, and marriage. Gandhi's father sold the land in order to support his wives, and his uncle was forced to migrate from the village after he divorced his second wife, the daughter of Saeed Zahraman. Her father came and told him to pay ten times the amount he owed him according to the marriage contract. He was accompanied by a group of armed men from his tribe and said he'd destroy Mashta Hasan and everyone in it. So his poor uncle was forced to sell the last two remaining pieces of land he owned, and paid, and took his wife and children and fled from the village. He went to live in Tripoli and never went back to the village except for brief visits.

And that day, during the burial of Husn, Little Gandhi's father, the uncle came to Gandhi. He was sitting beside him, scratching his nose and blowing it. Then he turned toward him and discussed his daughter with him. Gandhi agreed to marry her. He was twenty years old and wanted to start a new job. He came back, married the girl, and took her to Beirut.

The first day he was afraid of her as they rode in the taxi that took them to Halba, on the way to Beirut. He saw the whites of her eyes. He remembered the whites of the gypsy wife's eyes. He said to himself she'd kill him, and he'd be better off if he divorced her. But she stayed with him and gave him seven children. They all died before she had Husn and Suad. She wore him out with hospitals and the fear of her dying.

She was a silent woman. When he'd come home she'd sit quietly and not ask anything. She'd cook and clean, but she didn't care about anything. And Gandhi alone took on the difficult burden of their daughter.

Gandhi didn't remember much about Mashta Hasan.

"We don't own anything there," he said to me. "When you don't have any land, it doesn't have any meaning. Mashta Hasan is nothing to me. Even the house, we found out my father had mortgaged it . . . I don't know about the women, they went back to their villages, and the daughters got married, and I'm here."

Gandhi said he went once to the village after his father's death. "I went to see a distant cousin of mine, and there I found out the world had changed. The smell of apples filled the place. They stopped planting corn and wheat and planted apple trees. It was late August and the apples dangled from the trees, and their aroma wafted in the plain. From that day on I started loving apples, before then I didn't like them, to me they tasted like potatoes. I couldn't understand that American professor. I never saw him without an apple in his hand, chomping on it, while his books and notebooks nearly fell from his other hand. Now I love apples, the smell of them on the tree slices into your heart."

Gandhi remembered the story of the lira.

He remembered when he fled from the cave, that black night, and threw himself into the cornfields and walked, he remembered that he stopped in front of Haj Ismail's store and stole a lira from his cash register. Haj Ismail was a strange man. When he'd take the money from his customers, he'd tear the bills in half and put them in two separate piles on two sides of the register. That way no one could steal from him. When he wanted, he'd tape two halves back together. And so all the liras in the village had a piece of tape down the middle. The cash register was full of half-liras. Little Gandhi took two halves. He wasn't sure they were the same one; he was afraid to make sure and have Haj Ismail catch him as he fiddled with the register. And then again, how could he make sure when he couldn't even tell the face of the lira from the back side. He took the two halves and ran. He stuck them together with some glue he plucked from an almond tree and stopped a truck on the road to Halba. He waved the lira and the driver stopped. He let him ride in back between the sheaves of wheat and took him to Tripoli.

There, in the port, where the truck stopped, Gandhi saw the sea and was frightened. It was the first time in his life he saw something so huge, surging as it did, blue and colorful. He stood in front of the sea like an idiot, barely moving.

"Where are you headed?" the driver asked him.

"I don't know. Here."

"I'll take you to Rashid. You can work for him as an errand boy in the bakery."

Gandhi nodded his head in agreement and went to work there for four years. The first few months he slept at the bakery, then he moved to a room at Um Omar Hisiyyeh's house. He paid her ten piasters and two loaves of bread every day. Um Omar was deaf, but she never made a mistake counting her money and hid it in a place only she and God knew about. There were about ten young men who slept in that room.

Gandhi found work in Tripoli thanks to that glued-together lira. The driver was from the nearby village of Mashta Hammoud, and there was no question he'd told his father where he was. In the early days Gandhi was scared to death his father would come and kill him.

Master Baker Rashid's wife, Rashida, as Gandhi used to call her, put him at ease.

"Don't be afraid, you're with me, if he dares come I'll break his legs."

Gandhi was afraid, but his father didn't come and Gandhi didn't die. He stayed at the bakery for many long months, four years or more, and it was there he learned about life.

Master Rashid, the dark-skinned, gray-haired, slender man, looked like a key. That's what his wife, Um Jamal, used to say, the one Gandhi called Madame Rashida.

Madame Rashida was everything. She was in complete charge, while her husband the key did nothing. He'd sit in front of the oven, puffing away at the water pipe in front of him. Then he started running away from the bakery and going to the glass coffeehouse in Meena, where he'd spend the whole day puffing away and saying, "God help us." He talked a lot, and only about politics. He'd talk about the Ottoman sultans as though they were his own relatives. "How great was Sultan Abd al-Hamid; but they stabbed him in the back, woman." And the woman would sigh and tell him to worry about the price of flour. "Flour? What flour? You call this flour? You call this a country? You just don't understand." Then he'd go to his coffeehouse and wonder about this "Grand Liban" that was ultimately put together.

"Grand, my foot. May God make it smaller. What's so grand about it? We didn't want it that way. But what do we want anyway?"

That's what he did all day at the coffeehouse; he'd sit with a group of men puffing away at the water pipe and talking about how things had been turned upside down. They'd end up fighting over checker games, and when he'd return to the bakery tired at three in the afternoon, when Um Jamal was giving out the work orders for preparing the flour to make the night's dough, he'd come out of the blue with a question about political events and she'd shut him up with a wave of her hand. She'd dish out a plate of food for him. He'd eat in the bakery, sweat dripping from him, and then he'd go home to sleep. And Um Jamal ordered everyone around. Gandhi, who wasn't called Gandhi at the time (actually, they called him Abd), would stand there like a slave at her command. Abd would come hungry and exhausted after he finished delivering the packages of bread. She'd give him one loaf filled with yesterday's leftovers and two loaves for the deaf woman, and his daily earnings of half a lira. "Get going, God be with you, son," she'd tell him. Then she'd repeat the story of her son Jamal. "He's a loafer. He hates to work. But you, you're a real hard worker. I love you like a son. You're a little rascal." She'd look him up and down, as if she were trying to find out how much he made in tips from the houses he delivered bread to.

"I swear I don't have a piaster, Aunt, I'm broke."

Abd thought she was going to attack him to search through his pockets, but she didn't. She smiled, showing her yellow-black teeth and the gap that was left after two decayed teeth were extracted. "You're a son of a gun," she'd say to him. From that day on Gandhi was convinced he was a son of a gun. Otherwise, how would he have survived? No one could live in this country except a son of a gun.

He took a matchstick and struck it against his matchbox and began to whistle.

"It's ten piasters for an order of labneh, or there's no labneh," he said to the customers in his restaurant who were sitting on a stone bench in front of the door. He'd set down a glass of arak in front of him in his house in Nabaa, while around him sat a group of Kurdish and Hurani workers who'd become regular customers of this third-class restaurant Gandhi opened at the expense of Mr. Davis's dog. It had become very popular. The stone benches transformed into a real restaurant with cushions all over the floor.

"Those were the days," Gandhi said to the Reverend Amin, who stood before him like a statue, with his black shoes up on the shoe-shine box.

"Keep polishing, my son. God love you. You're a good boy. Why don't you come to church?"

"God forbid, Reverend. I believe in God," Gandhi would answer.

"Isn't the Church the house of God? Don't you know your Qur'an? 'And nearest among them in love to the Believers wilt thou find those who say "We are Christians" ' Come and take a look. What have you got to lose?"

And because Gandhi was a son of a gun, he decided to go and take a look.

The Reverend Amin wasn't a pastor of the formal and dignified Evangelical church located in Zuqaq al-Blat; rather, he led the parish of a small church on Makhoul Street. It was more like a house that had been converted into a church. The story of the Reverend Amin and his church was complicated. He was a real Reverend. He became one after studying history and theology at the American University and was appointed an itinerant pastor by the evangelical synod. Amin was a zealous young man. He took this appointment as being called on a mission for Christianity. He saw himself as one of Jesus' disciples, traveling throughout Lebanon and dying like the first martyrs. And so, on his way from Sidon to Beirut, Amin Aramouni discovered that the world belonged to him, and that he belonged to a future constructed out of knowledge and faith. That's what the American evangelists taught him with their wisdom and kindness. He came to the church from the depths of poverty. He believed that Christ's salvation meant the salvation of the whole world, and that America was the model of this new world that Christ had saved. He was twelve when famine struck Sidon during the First World War. The Reverend Amin didn't remember anything from those difficult years except the famine. He used to go with his father the cobbler to buy bread. He'd hold his father's hand firmly, because he was afraid his fast-paced father would leave him to the famine and have one less mouth to feed. On the sides of the streets of Sidon he'd see men and women with bloated bellies, screaming with hunger. That is when he learned not to give to anyone. He wasn't stingy, but he never gave. He learned you can't share your food with anybody, or you'll die. And when the Reverend Amin became a pastor in Ras Beirut, after the small schism that took place in the church of Beirut, he continued to feel that he had to hold on to each mouthful and couldn't share it with anyone. His wife, Eugenie, the Reverend Nabil Khoury's daughter, couldn't understand his stinginess. He was frugal about everything in the house except his whiskey. The children's clothes were the subject of many an argument. He'd travel through the various districts and come to Beirut at the beginning of the week to stay with his wife for a couple of days.

"I'm like a fisherman," he'd say to his wife. "I'm the fisher of souls. I go to locked-up churches and open them. I heal the sick, make the lame walk, and preach."

He'd take a bath and sit down with a bottle of whiskey, and he wouldn't get up until it was empty. His wife couldn't understand how a preacher could get drunk, for she was the daughter of a preacher and grew up inside the church. She never witnessed such drunkenness except in that house. But she didn't say anything. She saw in her husband the ghost of his father. She'd visited him once at their house in Ashrafiyyeh, before he died. She understood they belonged to a different milieu and a different world. Amin's father, Tannous al-Aramouni, was a tall man who limped and was cross-eyed. He lived in a country home in Ashrafiyyeh surrounded by China trees and a garden filled with loquat and almond trees, and one lone lemon tree and a tall palm tree. He was the only middle-aged man with no relatives, because his cousins, who lived in the village of Aramoun in the Aley area near Beirut, decided to cut off ties with him when he became a Protestant. But he had been forced into it. He told his wife if he hadn't become a Protestant he'd have died of starvation during World War I. But his wife went along with everything and went to that church that looked nothing like the churches she was accustomed to — there was not a single icon. She'd shut her eyes from that picture that made her want to laugh, and she'd pray like the others. At home, in a corner of her room, she kept a box of Byzantine icons. In front of the icons was an oil lamp whose wick burned night and day. She insisted on christening her children in the baptismal font at the monastery of Saint Elias Btina in Beirut. She brought the children one by one, all the way from Sidon to Beirut and immersed them in the font. She believed it would cure all illness and cleanse body and soul. Amin's mother hated Sidon and she couldn't understand how they got to be like that, but she was obedient to her husband. When he told her he'd changed his religion, she went along with it. He said she had to learn the new religion. She said she didn't have to, because all religions were the same to her. Whatever you want, she told her husband, is fine with me.

Her husband changed. Actually, nothing changed in him except the way he talked. Um Amin said to her half-senile mother-in-law that he'd started speaking Arabic with a quasi-classical manner, like the Palestinian Protestant pastor of the church in Sidon.

"If it hadn't been for my job at the American School I'd never have been able to send my kids to school. And if it hadn't been for this new Christian denomination, we'd have died of hunger, like dogs." Um Amin believed that all religions were similar, and she got used to the new one, but she never gave up making the sign of the cross like an Orthodox.

During her husband's last days, when Amin went to the American University to study theology and her second son, Nicholas, got a job in one of the hotels on Lake Tiberias, Um Amin went back to Beirut, leaving the rest of the family in Sidon. In Ashrafiyyeh, in the house she inherited from her father, Um Amin resumed her old relationships with family and neighbors. Abu Amin Aramouni's health deteriorated quickly and he became senile. He used to get lost in the streets of Ashrafiyyeh, thinking it was Sidon. He'd go to the coastal town of Dowra and sit for a long time thinking he was sitting at the port of Sidon. The woman was afraid her husband would get lost in the streets of Beirut, and Amin couldn't care less.

When Amin became a pastor, his mother's eyes were filled with tears, but his father, on the other hand, who'd been dressed up with a tie and all and was told to remove his fez in the church, was totally lost. Amin became a pastor and got married the same day. Um Amin gave her blessing.

"She's a nice girl. I wish you the best, my son. But tell her to speak to us in Arabic."

Eugenie, the Reverend Nabil Khoury's daughter, refused to visit the family in Ashrafiyyeh.

"Your mother talks too much," she said to him once.

Um Amin was the one who told Eugenie about his grandmother Um Tanios.

"Why did you tell her, Mom?"

"I wanted to entertain her, and she should know something about us," she said.

"She knows, but it was really unnecessary."

Um Amin told Eugenie the story of Um Tanios and how she became a Muslim saint.

She told her how Abu Amin tried to shut his mother up. Abu Hasan al-Hawwari came and kneeled at her feet and began kissing her. The delegations never stopped coming, and the cobbler didn't know what to do. When the woman died, al-Hawwari insisted on burying her in a Muslim cemetery. After long discussions and a lot of shouting, the two men came to an agreement. They performed the cleansing and shrouding for burial and then she was taken to Beirut, where she was buried in the family cemetery at Saint Mitr Church.

Um Tanios was eighty years old, living with her son and his family in their new house in Sidon. It was a one-story house with four rooms and a courtyard. The old woman lived in a room overlooking the courtyard. She was completely independent; she ate nothing but bread and water and never slept. She'd go often to the bathroom located on the edge of the courtyard. Night was a rhythm of footsteps pitter-pattering on the tiles of the courtyard. It was as if she never slept a wink.

Um Tanios didn't like Sidon and wanted to go back to Beirut. She'd laugh at her son when he told his small children to shut their eyes and pray before eating their meals. She'd sit all alone in front of the door to her room, even in the dead of winter, moving her lower jaw incessantly. After the First World War, she fell and broke her leg. After that she was unable to get out of bed, and she started forgetting things.

"It's senility," the doctor told her son.

"Impossible," Abu Amin said. "There is no history of senility in our family."

"She's got hardening of the arteries. There's nothing we can do."

She stayed in her bed for years. Um Amin took care of her while the old woman swore and moaned and went in and out of consciousness.

Then that strange thing happened.

It was about ten o'clock in the morning when this semiparalyzed woman began to shout in a loud voice, "O Muhammad, my Beloved."

Um Amin ran to her and found her sitting up in bed talking.

"A tall, dark young man, O Muhammad, my Beloved, let go of me, I want to get up. A young man, his mustache twirled upward, carrying a staff in his hand, stood beside me and poked me. He said to me, Um Tanios, stand up and walk. The end to your sorrow has come, my dear, you will get up. He poked me on the forehead with his staff, then on my stomach. He put the staff down and told me to get up. A young man, dark, tall, O Muhammad, my Beloved, let go of me, I want to get up, let go of me. Why have you tied me to the bed, he said to me, O my Beloved."

Um Amin screamed at her to shut up. But she went on, and her voice began to fade. She was covered with her own excrement as she tried to get up. She calmed her down, wiped her face with a wet cloth, and began washing her. The old woman wouldn't settle down. She'd push and shout, "My Beloved, dark and tall, you will get up, let go of me, I want to get up, O my Beloved, O Muhammad."

Um Amin heard footsteps out in the courtyard. She left the room and locked the door behind her only to find Abu Hasan al-Hawwari with a group of men standing in the middle of the courtyard.

"What's going on, neighbor?" al-Hawwari asked.

"Nothing. The woman is senile and she's screaming," said Um Amin.

"Have shame, woman of God. Cover your head and let us go see Mother."

"Who is Mother?" she asked.

"Um Tanios, Um Tanios saw the Prophet, peace be upon him, and we heard everything."

"Please, neighbor, leave me to my worries."

"Either you open the door or we'll break it down."

Um Amin went into the room. She left al-Hawwari and the men outside and went in. She locked the door behind her and pleaded with the old woman to quiet down, but the shouting was getting worse. Um Amin finished cleaning her and dressed her in her nightgown. She opened the door and went out.

When the old woman saw them she started screaming at the top of her lungs.

"My Beloved, O Muhammad, dark, tall, his mustache twirled upward, he had a staff with him, he poked me and said, You will get up." And she tried to get up. Al-Hawwari and Abu Lutfi took hold of her and stood her up, and she tried to walk.

Al-Hawwari told her son she walked. "I saw her. She stood up, I let go of her, and she walked. It's a miracle, dear Muhammad, Allahu Akbar."

The room turned into a shrine. The old woman's health was deteriorating and she had entered into a state of semiconsciousness. The visitors never stopped coming to see her. Women, children, men. And Um Amin never stopped making coffee.

"She has become a saint. She is indeed one of God's true saints," Sheikh Aiouti said after he left her room and kissed her hand. "Your house is blessed," he said to Abu Amin. "My son, this is the light of Islam, the light of dear Muhammad."

Abu Amin would nod his head, not knowing how to get out of this mess his mother had gotten him into. The problem wasn't solved until after the woman's death. She died suddenly. They got up in the morning and found her stone cold, she had been dead for hours. After a long discussion Sheikh Aiouti settled the matter. "We'll wash her;

you bury her." And that's what they did. They washed her and shrouded her amidst hymns and recitation of "La ilaha illa llah," and Abu Amin carried her to Beirut and buried her there. And with her he buried the story that, when Eugenie heard it from the Reverend Amin's mother, made her feel disgusted. She didn't like that kind of life.

She told her husband she felt he was different from the rest of his family.

She told her husband she felt that way, but he agreed with her. He agreed and lived with her all those years, always on her terms. She was everything; he was the wandering pastor, the nobody. When he'd get rid of the people around him he'd forget how to speak, and she'd have the final word. His only pleasure was the whiskey he drank the few nights he was home. The rest of his life was full of dust and traveling between Marjayoun and Sidon and Tyre and everyplace else. He'd return to that house in Beirut he inherited from his father-in-law, only to discover he was the head of a family he knew nothing about. His children spoke in English, and his wife cooked nothing but food you could hardly swallow. He made no objections. When he missed eating real food he'd flee to his mother's house, where he'd eat what he wanted and sleep till noon in his old bed.

The Reverend Amin was shocked by the obedience his wife displayed in front of his friends, especially the professors from the American University with whom he shared a special relationship. In front of them she was like a lamb. Mr. Davis envied him for this obedience in his wife and he'd say the magic of the East is its women. Perhaps it was because of this magic that Mr. Davis asked his friend the Reverend Amin to preach at the American University Church every Wednesday morning, which helped him a little financially.

Now the Reverend Amin had found himself all alone. His children had gone to the States, and Ms. Eugenie said she couldn't take the war and followed her children. And he was here. "A shepherd cannot leave his flock," he told his wife. But what flock? There was no longer a flock. He was the pastor of an empty church. Even his friendships fell apart, and his only friend, Lillian Sabbagha, had nothing to do with the church. "It was an innocent relationship," he said to Alice, who laughed and patted him on the shoulder.

"Don't worry about it, Reverend, don't worry," she said to him.

And on that incredible day there was a lot to worry about. Lillian Sabbagha stood in front of everyone like a lunatic and exposed their relationship. That day the Reverend didn't dare leave the house. He walked behind the coffin of Vitsky the maid, but he was obliged not to enter the church because people's eyes pierced his back like needles.

The Reverend Amin had no idea why Lillian would say such a thing. She stood inside Vitsky's room and started blabbing like a madwoman. Once she caught sight of him she started talking, and she didn't stop until Father John interfered. Why did she do it? Did she hate him, or was she crazy, or was it that she couldn't take it anymore and had to tell everything?

"It was a lie," he told Alice, who didn't believe him. The Reverend Amin was alone and sad. There was no one left. If it hadn't been for Alice taking care of him now and then, he'd have become a laughingstock, a useless beggar.

But why did she say what she said? Why did she ridicule him and turn him into a joke?

Was it because he asked her to fly? The Reverend

Amin didn't want to sleep with her, and even if he had wanted to he couldn't. Ever since Eugenie left he couldn't.

"Unfaithfulness requires the presence of the wife. When the wife disappears, or leaves the country, unfaithfulness loses its meaning."

Alice looked at him sympathetically, for she'd heard this kind of talk hundreds of times. But she couldn't figure out how he wanted to make her fly.

"Is it true, Reverend? Did you really want to make her fly?"

The Reverend Amin slipped into a state of lethargy, laughed, and didn't answer.

"But how, though, how did you think she was going to fly? Did you want to throw her from the window?"

The Reverend Amin didn't want to throw her from the window, or the door, or anywhere else for that matter. Once he told Alice he'd tell the truth, but on condition she not tell a soul.

"My heart is like a deep well; you can trust me, my friend."

He said he went to her house as usual, that he'd started visiting her a while back. Then the visits turned into a regular thing. He went to her house and Vitsky, her maid, was getting ready to leave. Her demented daughter was asleep in her room. He sat in the living room and drank a beer with her, for she didn't allow him to drink whiskey because she couldn't stand the smell. They sat together and talked. She was asking him to retell the story of his grandmother Um Tanios with the Prophet Muhammad. He told her the story and she laughed hysterically. "I moved close to her," he said. "I only wanted to put my head on her chest. I like that. With Eugenie I used to lay my head on her chest and say 'Mama' to her. She'd answer me, 'Daddy,' and run her fingers through my hair as we watched television. I wanted Eugenie, and so I put my head on Lillian's chest, and instead of saying 'Daddy' to me and running her fingers through my hair, she got up, grabbed me by the hand, and took me to her room. She took off her blouse and her brassiere and I saw those two large breasts. I didn't do anything. I approached her. I held her by the hand and sat her down on the edge of the bed. I sat down next to her and placed my head on her chest. But she stood up again. She ran and turned off the light. She stood in front of the window, next to the windowsill, as if she was going to fall out. She was leaning forward with her hands on the windowsill, and her hair flowed over her breasts. I was afraid she'd fall and die. I ran to her. The room was dark, and so I tripped over the chair and fell to the floor. She stayed in front of the window, motionless. I got up and grabbed her by the waist and tried to bring her back to the bed, but she refused. I didn't tell her to fly. She said she wanted to fly. I didn't say any of what was said about me. All I did was put my head on her chest and nearly start to cry. But she's crazy. She's the crazy one. It would happen every time after that. She'd take off her blouse and her bra and stand next to the window. That whole story of flying, and that I would push the woman and ask her to fly is just not true."

Lillian Sabbagha told quite a different story.

She said the Reverend tried to rape her. She went to the priest, Father John, kneeled before him in the confessional, and told him whatever came to her mind. Father John didn't say anything to her. He knew she wasn't completely balanced mentally, that she spoke illogically, and that the whole affair was shameful. Did it make sense that the poor Reverend would push her from the window and rape her? It seemed the woman had lost her mind since the death of her white Russian maid.

In that maid Little Gandhi saw the image of the white angel. She'd pass by him, with that head of hers, which was always held high, and that back, which never bowed down to anyone. And she'd tell him to come and get the shoes. Never once did she bring him a single shoe. She'd stand next to him without looking down where he was sitting next to his shoe-shine box, in front of the row of shoes lined up on the sidewalk. Gandhi would leave everything and go to pick up Madame Lillian and her maid's shoes. The maid's shoes were cleaner and more elegant than the madame's.

Gandhi had no idea this woman was a Russian princess and that she worked for the Sabbagha family after she sold all the jewelry she'd brought with her from Russia. She was fifteen and had crossed continents and countries only to find herself in the port of Beirut, not Alexandria. She tried to find work, and she did, teaching French to local Beiruti children. But she was like someone who's always waiting for something. Only Father John al-Mazraani knew the real story about her, and during mass he insisted on beginning Communion with her. She would stand first in line, wearing her white robe and orange sash, and the priest would bow to her with his chalice.

Madame Sabbagha was the one who let out the secret to everyone in the neighborhood. That was the day she found Vitsky dead in her small room. Madame Sabbagha shrieked and said, "The princess, the daughter of princes." The neighbors came running. Abu Saeed al-Munla, Spiro with the hat, the teacher Ahmad, Husn, Dr. Atef, Alice, Zaylaa, and lots of women. They were all in front of the house. And when Lillian Sabbagha heard one of the women asking "What's wrong with the maid?" she shouted "You, you're the servants; this was a princess."

The white princess was dead inside the house, sprawled out on her bed in her white nightgown, as if she'd known she was going to die. Her eyes were shut and her hands were folded together over the blankets. There was a faint smell of decay coming from the room.

Father John ordered everyone out and everyone went out except Madame Sabbagha. Then the doctor came and declared that the death had occurred at night, the cause being a heart attack.

Father John carried out the burial rites right away, but Madame Sabbagha insisted on having the bishop come and started screaming in the priest's face. Everyone was at the house, which had suddenly filled up with nuns. Gandhi didn't know where the nuns had come from, or how they'd entered the princess's room. Everyone was in the entrance, which had been turned into a reception area, and the priest was saying there was a war going on and it was impossible for the bishop to come. And Madame Sabbagha screamed and wailed. Here the Reverend Amin stepped in and the scandal broke out. She attacked him, Gandhi said, and almost killed him. She shouted that he wanted to kill her and tried to rape her and throw her from the window. At that point, Gandhi said, Father John stopped the commotion and scooted the Reverend out the door. He promised Lillian he'd get in touch with the bishop.

The next day the bishop crossed the green line and came to the burial.

Alice told me that Father John al-Mazraani told her the whole story.

"Unbelievable. You know how it is. You must know. Things have a way of turning around with the passing of time. And this Russian woman was the turning point. Life didn't turn around, she did. Oh, I don't know."

Alice said her friendship with Father John al-Mazraani began because she was concerned about the Reverend Amin during his last days. After she brought him to the nursing home in Ashrafiyyeh, Father John became her friend. She'd visit him in the late afternoon as he sat on the bench of Our Lady Church, drinking lemonade and telling her about Mary Magdalene. And she'd tell him about her life.

He asked her once why she didn't come to church on Sundays.

"How can I, Father? I'm a Muslim."

"A Muslim? I can't believe it. You look like you could've studied at the nuns' school."

"I was a student of the whorehouse. It's all the same, Father."

The priest had become convinced that it really was all the same. There he was, living alone and isolated. His beard was going gray and the long hair he kept tied in a bun at the back of his neck was falling out. And the days passed, and the war took everyone away. There was no one left. They were all gone. Life now meant waiting for death. Father John, the priest of the Orthodox Church of Beirut, now felt that it was all the same in the end. Had he stayed in Hawsh Malab al-Salaam and become a soccer player, he'd have wound up exactly the same as he was now.

As a child he was ashamed of the "Hawsh" and he wasn't really a Mazraani. It was the old senile Bishop Athanasios, God rest his soul, who stuck his family with the name "Mazraani" (Farmer). Father John, whose real name was Anwar Nasri, was born in Hawsh Malab al-Salaam. There he was born with hundreds of children, in stone shacks that were built next to the soccer field in Ashrafiyyeh in order to accommodate the Hurani immigrants who left the Suweida region in the 1920s during the great

Syrian Revolution. People fled to Beirut. Women in long black robes, black headdress braided over their heads, tattoos covering their hands and chins, and behind them the children and the men. In Beirut, the men did construction work and the women worked as maids in people's homes. They all lived in the Hawsh, which belonged to the Greek Orthodox Endowment Fund of the Beirut Diocese. Here Anwar Nasri was born and received a free education. His mother took him to the diocese because he had a beautiful voice. He lived in that luxurious building in the Sursuq Quarter of West Beirut. He ate like a king, studied theology, and carried the censer until he became a priest.

"I didn't have the luck to become a bishop. Maybe it was because they saw me as just the son of a maid. Isn't a maid a human being, too? Shame on them. But it's better this way. My responsibilities are few, Alice. This way I'll stand before Him with double the talents He gave me, and I won't be scoffed at in the next world."

From Ashrafiyyeh he went to Ras Beirut, and there he has lived for thirty years. He'd seen everything. He saw the city as it was being transformed into the Tower of Babel. He saw people speaking all languages, and he saw the faces as they turned into ruins of time. He'd seen it all, and now he sat on the stone bench, a glass of lemonade in his hand, aching with loneliness and listening to Alice's memoirs and the stories of his neighbors, wanting a woman. Any woman. Our Father John had started confusing women in his mind, mixing names and faces, uncertain about who goes with what and where to begin. He'd see them before him like shadows coming and going, totally elusive to him. All the pleasures of this world had gone. Cholesterol and high blood pressure, there was only one pleasure that remained, words. Talking was the only delight Father John al-Mazraani couldn't get enough of. He'd sit out in front of his church like a hunter waiting for his prey to be caught in the snare of his words.

That was how he told everyone the story of poor Vitsky, and each time he exaggerated the details a little bit.

When he told the story to Abu Saeed, he added the part about Vitsky's infatuation with him, and how his priest's habit prevented him from committing a sin. The priest was making things up of course, for Vitsky never met him at the diocese. The last time she visited the diocese, when the scandal with Bishop Athanasios took place, she was twenty years old. Father John was still a child playing soccer in Malab al-Salaam. He said she fell in love with him, and until this day he still has a special place in his heart for her. That's why he insisted the bishop attend the funeral, even though Abu Saeed had seen him screaming at Lillian, telling her it would be impossible.

Father John was convinced of what he told. We're all like that. We believe in what we say. And when I try to write what they told me, I discover that Alice was right.

"Memories are a disgrace, my son. Once you get to the point where there's nothing left but your memories, it's over. The mule has stopped pulling for you, and the lantern's on its last drop of oil."

Vitsky was scared when Simaan Fayyad drove her to Lillian Sabbagha's house. Lillian was living with her daughter Sorayya and her husband, George. Vitsky agreed with Lillian to come every day to help with the housework, but she refused to sleep at the house. Mr. George helped her find a room to rent at the end of Makhoul Street, the very room in which the white princess died.

Vitsky was not a maid in every sense of the word. Actually, there was an elderly maid called Wadia at Madame Sabbagha's house. Vitsky was the caretaker. She spoke only French. She decided which foods were to be cooked and would not tolerate anyone questioning her orders. She despised that Lebanese bourgeoisie, which could fathom only the outer skin of civilization.

After Mr. George died of leukemia, and the daughter was sent to a school for the handicapped in the village of Beit Miri, a strong friendship grew between the maid and the mistress. The mistress thrived on the past glories of the Sabbagha family, and the maid refused to tell anything about Russia and the czars. The maid was the true mistress. She acted as though the house belonged to her, and as though Madame Lillian was living in her house. The main thing that bothered Vitsky was her feeling that she'd come to Beirut against her will. She'd fled to Istanbul with her cousin Philip, who was an officer in the White Army. Vitsky always insisted on calling it Constantinople after the occupation of the family castle in Kiev. She fled with her cousin without knowing anything about the true fate of the rest of her family. One of the emigrant White Russians who surrounded Istanbul told her they were all killed. From Istanbul they'd decided to immigrate to Alexandria. Her cousin made the decision, and she went along with it. Vitsky believed they'd get married in Alexandria. Her cousin disappeared. He left her in the small hotel on a street whose name she didn't know. He left and didn't come back. She waited ten days for him and then boarded the ship that took her to Beirut rather than Alexandria.

In Beirut she found nowhere to go but the diocese. There she found herself among a group of immigrants who'd been given makeshift accommodations. Vitsky lived there in a small room with no windows near Akawi hill and began giving private French lessons in people's homes.

She told Madame Lillian she preferred teaching.

Madame Sabbagha smiled wickedly. She didn't tell her

her daughter was disturbed, but that she was at a boarding school and Vitsky could tutor her during the summer.

And Vitsky became a maid, thanks to Simaan Fayyad, who saved her from that strange situation she found herself in when Bishop Athanasios tried to sleep with her.

In this white young woman, the bishop saw the features of kings.

"You look like the czars," he said to her.

And she always denied having any relation to the Romanov family. She said she was of noble blood and that her fiancé was an officer in the Royal Army.

"You're being modest," the bishop said, refusing to believe her.

The bishop fell in love with this young woman. He'd take her with him to visit the richest families in Beirut, where he'd arrange for her to work as a tutor for their daughters.

Every evening the bishop would invite her to evening prayers. He always prayed at 4:30 in the evening, in the small church in the diocese. At 4:15 she'd find Simaan Fayyad waiting for her at the door to her room. He'd walk her to the parish, and there she'd join in the prayer in a language she didn't understand. Once she said the prayer of Zakariyya. She said it in French, her voice trembling. "Now release your slave, O Master, according to your word, in peace." And when she reached the word *peace,* when Zakariyya asks God to kill him, she stopped chanting and her voice was drowned with sobs. The tears rolled down her face, and the deacons who were attending the prayers were struck with amazement and sorrow.

That day "His Eminence" made her stay for dinner, and after dinner he took her to the reading room, and there he tried to sleep with her. Vitsky didn't say anything, not knowing Arab customs. It never occurred to her that this

114

old man in his seventies would try what her young officer fiancé never tried.

He pulled her toward him and kissed her on the forehead. The smell of old wood, like the smell of icons, permeated the reading room. And His Eminence Athanasios with his white beard, short stature, and neck that shook from side to side, diffused an aroma like the smell of wood. When he kissed her forehead she was taken by the smell, as though she'd surrendered to him. So he pushed her against the wall. She stood, not understanding what was happening, and he went after her. Just like that, with no introductions, he started kissing her face. She began to scream and so he put his hand over her mouth. She threw her arms up to push him away, and then she ran. She couldn't find the door; the dim light made it difficult for her to see. She ran and fell onto the floor. There he was, on top of her in his black priest's gown, trying to pin her down. The sound of him panting rang in her ears. She slid out from under him using her elbows and stood up. She found the door in front of her, opened it, and ran out.

In the courtyard she noticed the blood.

The edge of her olive-colored dress was covered with blood. She bent down, overcome with grief, and found a deep cut on her right knee. Simaan Fayyad offered her his arm without saying a word. She held on to the man's arm and went back to her room.

Whenever Vitsky got sad and when the anxiety of waiting for her fiancé who never came back took hold of her, and memories brought her to the brink of regret, she'd uncover her knee to show Lillian Sabbagha the scar that would never disappear. She'd tell her there was only one place she wanted to be buried, in Kiev, in Holy Russia.

Madame Sabbagha would try to soothe her by telling her she reserved a plot for her among the Sabbagha family graves and that she'd be buried next to the noblest family in Beirut.

"We are the seven families, my dear, and you will be buried with one of the great families. As if you were at home."

Madame Sabbagha would start telling the story while knitting with some blue yarn and blue knitting needles, sitting in the middle of the living room. Vitsky sat with her, listening with half an ear. Madame Sabbagha wouldn't turn on the lights until it got completely dark inside. But during the early hours of the evening, when light mixes with darkness, Vitsky could no longer see anything but the open loops in the yarn, for Madame Sabbagha refused to turn on the lights.

"I'm not stingy, but why do we need the lights when we can still see? It's a waste."

"You're right," Vitsky would say, yawning. She'd say in broken Arabic she'd had it and was going to bed. Vitsky would speak Arabic when she wanted to express dissatisfaction, as if this language was good only for swearing and expressing dissatisfaction.

Madame Sabbagha would go on knitting the blue sweater she would never send to her grandson, because her daughter never got married and didn't live in France. Her daughter, whom she never visited, was in the sanitarium in Dayr al-Salib. She told everyone she sent her to France and she got married there. She said she was knitting for her grandson little George.

Vitsky wanted to go, but Madame Sabbagha tried to make her stay and listen to her stories about the past glories of her family, now extinct.

"It's unbelievable. They all died. I'm the only one left. I'm like you, Vitsky. I'm all alone. I have no one."

"No, not you. Me, yes. You know who I am."

"Of course I know. But they're all dead. One was a lawyer, one was a journalist, and one was a poet. Three brothers. The first got married but didn't have any children. The second never married, he just kept on chasing after barmaids. The third died a young man, eighteen years old. His name was Shukri. He was really something, as beautiful as a full moon on a clear day. He died of typhus at eighteen, and only I remained. And I, too, had only a daughter. They married me off to my cousin in order to keep the money in the family. As you know, he was, God rest his soul, a bit simpleminded. He spent his time selling the land we inherited, and then he laid down his head and died. They all died, leaving no male descendants to carry on the family name. Shukri drove the Jesuits crazy. Once the class was supposed to write a poem, and so Shukri wrote twenty poems for the whole class, using twenty different meters and twenty different rhyme schemes. His poem was the best; it drove the Jesuit priests crazy. 'Don't trust a Jesuit priest / who dons a demon's habit / And saunters in it like a he-goat in his lair' or his hair or his I don't know what. Poor me. I was the only one who didn't have a good memory. To hell with memory; it eats you alive and makes a laughingstock out of you."

She'd repeat the same stories every evening. How Wadia the maid died and was transferred to her distant village in Akkar. Curses against the war and those fighting in it. Stories about the hairdresser, and Madame Nuha Aoun, who was killed. All this with Vitsky at her side, like her own sister.

Simaan Fayyad told Vitsky that Madame Sabbagha would be like a sister to her. He told her he'd rescue her from the mess with the bishop and take her to work in Ras Beirut at the Sabbagha residence, and the madame will be like more than a sister to you.

After that Simaan Fayyad disappeared.

Vitsky spoke about him once in front of Madame Sabbagha. She said he was a gentleman, and very sweet, and so Madame Sabbagha broke into laughter.

"He's an idiot, my friend. I hope you didn't fall in love with him."

Vitsky shuddered at talk about love. She never loved anyone. Her whole life she remained faithful to the Russian officer whom she searched for everywhere. For twenty years or so she'd go to the Red Cross in Beirut and inquire about him. Then she stopped going because the official there started treating her as if she were crazy. Vitsky was never in love with that nitwit Simaan Fayyad. All she said was that he was cute.

Simaan Fayyad really was a nitwit. Everyone treated him like one and he couldn't do anything right. He wasted his father's fortune with the stroke of a pen after one of his uncles convinced him to take him as his partner in the silk business. The business evaporated and along with it the fortune. Simaan Fayyad then became a sexton in Saint George's Cathedral in the middle of town and put in time every evening at the diocese doing nothing.

It was Simaan Fayyad who told Vitsky that Russia was the salt of the earth. He told her the story of his grandfather. Prince Alexander, the czar's brother, visited Beirut in 1896 and roamed around in the Sursuq Quarter, where his grandfather Fayyad Fayyad lived and worked as a silk merchant.

He told about how the czar's brother rode around Beirut in a carriage drawn by six Arabian horses. When he got to the Sursuq Quarter he saw a strange thing. There was a mound of salt on the side of the road roughly five meters long and two meters wide. Hundreds of lighted candles had been placed on top of it. And Mr. Fayyad Fayyad stood there next to it wearing his red fez and his white silk gown with the striped belt. He stood in front of the candles, waiting, as though he were guarding them.

The czar's brother stopped the carriage, which was being pulled by six pure-bred Arabian horses, got out, and saw Fayyad.

"What is this?" asked the blond Russian prince with the gleaming blue eyes.

Fayyad Fayyad bowed down so low his tarboosh nearly touched the ground and said, "This is for His Highness the Prince."

He asked the interpreter accompanying him what it meant.

Fayyad stood up straight and said, "Salt. Salt means Russia is the salt of the earth."

The interpreter translated Fayyad's words into Russian. The czar's brother approved with a big smile that made his whole face shine.

"And the candles?" the prince asked.

"The candles, Your Majesty, the candles symbolize Russia as the light of the world," Fayyad said without waiting for the interpreter to translate the prince's question into Arabic.

After the interpreter translated Fayyad's answer into Russian the prince approached this Lebanese man, placed his hand on his head, and said, "Demand whatever you want, I speak on behalf of the czar of Russia. The czar of all Russia takes you under his protection, and is ready to grant all your requests. Demand whatever you want. All your wishes will be granted."

Fayyad Fayyad listened to the prince's words through the voice of the interpreter, his eyes watching the prince and not believing what they saw.

The old man with the wrinkled face couldn't decide what to ask for, and so he stood there silently, as though he hadn't heard the Russian prince's words.

"Say something, Uncle," the interpreter said.

Fayyad Fayyad said he had one request.

"What is your request?" the interpreter asked, as though he were trying to get Fayyad to hurry up and say something.

"My request, my son, tell His Highness, tell him, I don't want them to tell me 'Throw the rope down, Fayyad' anymore."

"What do you mean?" the interpreter said.

"You tell him that every evening, this guy who lights up the streets comes. I'd be sitting in my house on the first floor and he comes and says, 'Throw the rope down, Fayyad' and I throw it down. I fill the lantern with oil, raise it back up with the rope, hang it up, and light it. I don't want anyone to tell me, 'Throw the rope down, Fayyad' anymore."

Fayyad Fayyad didn't know what the interpreter translated to the czar's brother. All he saw was the prince's smile beaming on his face. His face twinkled like an icon. The czar's brother got in his carriage drawn by six pure-bred Arabian horses and left Fayyad and his candles lighted all night long.

Vitsky asked if Fayyad stopped letting down the lantern, and Fayyad the grandson answered, "I don't know. The Turks left and then came the French, and under the French everything changed. The Jesuits took over everything and we no longer knew in which country we were living. One minute the state of Beirut, the next Greater Lebanon, the next Syria, and the next I don't know what. The French are like priests; no one understands them."

Simaan Fayyad was trying to explain to the Russian princess that the French mandate was the cause of all the problems. But she didn't quite understand his position, for he loved France and loved to sleep.

Vitsky no longer saw Simaan Fayyad after her arrival at the Sabbagha family house. But she used to say that all the Lebanese are like Fayyad, they don't know what they're asking for and they don't know what they want. She especially hated the Reverend Amin and refused to talk to him. She'd look at him with disgust when he'd come to visit Madame Sabbagha. She'd go into a small room next to the kitchen and turn on the television.

The Reverend Amin didn't try to speak to her. He knew she hated him, and he didn't like her either. He saw her as the main obstacle in his new relationship with Lillian Sabbagha.

The Reverend Amin was lonely. From the time his wife left he felt sad, and as if the world were slipping out from under him. His church had become empty; no one came to it anymore. He, too, decided not to pray there. He'd pray in his house, all alone. He'd read the Bible but wouldn't give any sermons. He felt his throat was dry and he needed a lot of whiskey. He'd find himself alone in front of Our Lady Church, and Father John would drive him home.

Gandhi told Alice senility had eaten up the Reverend Amin's brain, that he could no longer speak normally. He spit more than he talked.

And Alice would smile. "That's life," she'd say. "Who'd have said that all glory reverts to clay in the end."

No one remembered how the Reverend Amin used to be, how he opened his church and built his parish single-handedly.

The Reverend Amin told her, and Alice believed him.

He said he'd lost hope when he wasn't elected to be pastor of Beirut after the Reverend Fuad Tahhan's death. It was then, in 1963, that Alfred came. Alfred was an eccentric man. They said he'd been involved with the unsuccessful military coup attempt undertaken by the Syrian Socialist Party in 1961, and that after a year in prison he worked as an officer in the Secret Service (Deuxième Bureau). Alfred wanted to marry the Reverend Amin's daughter Samia, but she refused because she was in love with an American student with a red beard who was planning to marry her and take her to California. Alfred was the one who encouraged the Reverend Amin to establish an independent church in Ras Beirut. He rented the house and gathered the parishioners and convinced Dr. John Davis to be the first. Alfred Sawaya was in his forties, bald, with protruding eyes and protruding red lips.

Alfred came to the first church meeting and said a pastor must be elected. He announced his own nomination and started campaigning about his virtues, and about his grandfather who was the first in Lebanon and Syria to embrace the Protestant faith.

The church would have slipped out of Amin Aramouni's hands had John Davis not settled the matter. The tall American stood up in the middle of the small hall, which was full of men and women, and spoke in Arabic.

"It's not right," he said. "You are an officer, Mr. Alfred, and an officer doesn't have the right to be a pastor. We want Reverend Amin."

Amin expected Alfred to defend himself, but he didn't speak. He left the church and didn't come back. And from that day on the Reverend Amin became the respected and cherished pastor of the Presbyterian Church of Ras Beirut.

Amin never forgot that he began his life as a missionary and that his duty was to minister to non-Christians.

And so he found in Little Gandhi what he'd been searching for.

Gandhi had closed his restaurant for good after the death of the dog and went back to the shoe-shine business. He'd put his box in front of Faysal's Restaurant and start working at six in the morning. He was, with his loose-fitting clothes and his head bent over his box, the main guidepost in the street. He was the shoe shiner everyone went to. He worked quietly and carefully; you could barely hear his voice. When he spoke, he'd whisper and wave his hands, as if he thought his voice came out of his hands. His customers didn't understand a word he said, but they came anyway. Business was booming for him, especially after the Reverend decided to include him in his little church and the whole congregation started going to him.

Gandhi told Alice they were a strange bunch of people.

He told her the Reverend's followers were a bunch of idiots, smiling all the time.

"They always want to prove how happy they are."

Gandhi was pleased with them. A never-ending supply of shoes and smiles. He'd smile back at them, but always with some hesitancy. He didn't quite know what to do in order not to spoil their happiness for them. Should he smile, or listen, or pretend he was completely wrapped up in his work?

They'd come, stand with their shoes on his shoe-shine box, and talk incessantly. They'd ask him about his work and his children and he'd answer them as best he could. Gandhi spoke about that blond bearded man in particular, who never stopped asking questions. He'd ask him about his village, his father, his grandfather, his opinion about Beirut.

"I don't know anything," Gandhi would answer.

"This is exactly what I'm interested in," the man said. "I'm very interested in simplicity; philosophy these days is all about discovering simplicity."

He started visiting Gandhi at his humble house and eating with him. He'd sit on the wooden bench inside his small house, talking and asking questions.

"I look for life wherever I can find it."

The blond bearded man told everyone he had discovered the simple life through Gandhi, that Gandhi was like Jesus, and that the poor were the salt of the earth.

Once Gandhi was in church.

Gandhi didn't know why he agreed with the Reverend Amin to go to church. He was a "son of a gun," as he said, but that wasn't enough justification for going. Maybe this young bearded man attracted him with his simplicity and his womanlike tenderness; or maybe it was that he wanted to see how they prayed; or because he thought there couldn't be any danger in the matter; or because he couldn't find a good reason not to.

"No problem," he said to the Reverend Amin.

"Sunday, nine o'clock," the Reverend said.

"Sunday," Gandhi answered.

Gandhi sat in the back and didn't understand a thing. He watched while they chanted and shook their heads and bodies. "It's like watching TV," he said to Alice. And suddenly the show ended. They all sat down as the Reverend Amin closed his eyes and began to pray. Soon afterward, the bearded fellow climbed up to the pulpit and spoke about simplicity. The Reverend Amin was sitting in an aisle seat and the bearded man stood, giving his sermon and pointing up with his index finger. His sermon was in perfect classical Arabic, half of which was lost on Gandhi. His voice was shaking and you could see the veins in his neck popping out. His hand went up and down as he said,

"Blessed are the meek." Everyone sat in their seats muttering "hmmm" as if they understood.

"Blessed are the poor in spirit, for theirs is the kingdom of heaven. / Blessed are those who mourn, for they shall be comforted. / Blessed are the meek, for they shall inherit the earth. / Blessed are those who hunger and thirst after righteousness, for they shall be filled. / Blessed are the merciful, for they shall obtain mercy. / Blessed are the pure in heart, for they shall see God. / Blessed are . . . "

He'd say "blessed" and point with his finger, and the heads would turn to the back where Gandhi was sitting. Gandhi felt like a dog and soon found himself leaving the church. Their glances pierced through his face, and so he got scared and went out of the church, leaving the bearded young man on the pulpit caught up in his own words.

Gandhi told the Reverend Amin he had gotten scared.

The Reverend laughed. "Don't worry about it," he said, putting his foot up on the shoe-shine box. "That young man is very zealous. He doesn't know how he should speak. God forgive him."

"God forgive everyone, but tell him to get off my back."

"Be patient, man," the Reverend said.

"God grant you a long life, Reverend. You all speak English. I don't understand a word. What's-his-name starts speaking Arabic like he's speaking English. I don't understand a word, I . . . "

Gandhi laughed and his hands finished the sentence for him.

The Reverend Amin agreed. He wanted Gandhi, but he hated this sort of simplicity the Americans are good at putting on. He hated simplicity when it came to his wife, Eugenie, for she always spoke cautiously, twisting her jaws in order to prevent the letter *alef* from sounding mellow the way everyone in Beirut pronounced it. She'd lower her voice and put her hand over her mouth to hide her smile. Yet, in spite of her meekness and simplicity, she hated the poor, despised them. As for the Reverend Amin, he hadn't visited his brothers and sisters for some time. His mother had died, and his cobbler brother had immigrated to Saudi Arabia. His second brother fled from Tiberias when Palestine fell and lived in the family house. Madame Eugenie, however, didn't care for him or his wife and children, because they were like poor people's children.

Amin agreed, for he no longer knew how to talk to his brother, or any of his relatives for that matter. He'd become like his wife's family, raising the *alef* and speaking English and forgetting.

Gandhi told the Reverend Amin to forget it. "Forget the whole thing. If you don't want me, I'll pick up my shoeshine box and go. God's world is a big place, you know."

The Reverend Amin didn't say anything. He told him not to go and explained about the bearded young man and why the people got mad at him.

"This guy had just come from America. He studied philosophy and wanted to prove how smart he was."

"But I can't," Gandhi said.

"You're right, my son. I can't either. Don't be upset."

Gandhi agreed to forgive the bearded young man and forgive him his sins, and to stop spitting on the ground whenever he saw him walking in the streets.

The bearded young man was a spy. That's what Madame Nuha Aoun told him as she gave him her black-and-white shoe with the perforations; the one Gandhi had such a hard time polishing and would save for the end so he could take his time with it.

"He's a spy, Mr. Gandhi," Nuha said. "They're all

126

spies. But their days are numbered. Soon France will come to our rescue and save us from all this garbage."

Gandhi wasn't sure if she was talking about the Reverend Amin and his friends or the Americans who were all over Bliss Street with their shorts and their dogs.

All of that was over. Time passed by all of them like the blinking of an eye. The Americans left and the Reverend Amin started wetting his pants, and his church had been transformed into a warehouse for al-Munla and his gang. Zaylaa was the one who made the decision. After everything was stolen from the church immediately after an armed battle between the various organizations in the area on the fifth and sixth of June 1980, which led to a lot of destruction, misfortune, and looting, Zaylaa, who was king of the hill, decided the church could be used for a number of purposes. He gave it to al-Munla to use as a storage space for clothes Abu Saeed was importing from Hong Kong and Taiwan and selling as European goods.

Alice said the Reverend's condition had deteriorated strangely. She said she saw him the previous Sunday—that was Sunday, the seventh of July, 1980. The Reverend Amin walked aimlessly in the streets. His pants were dirty and nearly falling off of him. He walked, carrying a black book. I saw him, she said. I saw him open the door of the church with his long key and go in. He left the door open and walked over the piles of pants and shirts. He stopped in front of the pulpit, opened his book, and started reading things about Jerusalem and the prophets.

"O Jerusalem, Jerusalem, thou that killest the prophets and stonest them which are sent unto thee, how often would I have gathered thy children together, even as a hen gathereth her chickens under her wings, and ye would not!

"Behold, your house is left unto you desolate. For I

say unto you, ye shall not see me henceforth, till ye shall say, Blessed is he that cometh in the name of the Lord."

He read and read, and his voice was very soft. His face hung loose and his legs quivered. He sat as if he were falling onto the edge of his old pulpit and started to cry. That was after the whole thing with Lillian Sabbagha, and after everyone had gone. Alice said she went in, took him by the hand, and tried to lead him home. But he walked to the front of Our Lady Church and there he held onto the railing as if he didn't want to let go. He started praying in a loud voice.

From that day on, the man started falling apart. He became delirious and spent most of his time inside Our Lady Church. Father John tried to calm him down and asked Alice to take him home. Only Alice was left; she took him herself to the nursing home and returned with a pallid face and eyes swollen from crying so much.

In the Salonica Hotel, Alice burst into a fit of laughter and the Egyptian owner thought she'd gone crazy.

"What's happened to you, Alice?"

"I'm laughing at myself, and this world. Who's going to be there to take care of me when it's my turn?"

No one took care of her. When the war broke out again on February 6, 1984, and the business district transformed into a theater of destruction, Alice disappeared. We didn't hear anything about her. Did she die, or did she go to some unknown place? Did someone take care of her, or was she left, alone, in the middle of the destruction?

Whenever Alice talked about her memories, she'd lean on her right hand and let herself slip away. I saw her, and she was always like that. When she spoke she'd slip away to I don't know where.

"Life is like the bracelet, my son. When he came with the scissors to cut the bracelet, I laughed. He got the scissors and broke it. When I saw it there on the ground, I broke into tears, and he started laughing. I was young and didn't know anything. He was laughing and I was standing in front of him, crying. He told me that's enough, get up, take a shower and get dressed, we have to go. I took a shower and got dressed and went, and I'm still going. His name was Abu Jamil. An impresario, you know, the guy who works everything out. He'd talk to the nightclub owner and fix the price; his word was final. I went when he cut the bracelet. Life is like the bracelet. Look. Look right now and tell me what you see."

She raised her hand up, and I heard a rattling sound. I saw the black sleeve roll down over her wrist, revealing a collection of silver bracelets, some thin, some wide.

"I sold all my bracelets and bought new ones. This place "The Montana," it's not a bar, it's a whorehouse. And Zaylaa isn't anywhere near al-Askary. And men these days aren't men. And I am not myself. Get up, my son, get up. You never told me who you were, who your father is."

I was sitting with her in her room at the Salonica Hotel. The walls were red and peeling so badly they looked as though they hadn't been scraped for a thousand years. She was sitting on the edge of the only bed, which was plopped in the middle of the empty room. Next to her was a small kerosene stove she used for making coffee and boiling potatoes. I was sitting on a chair stripped of its bamboo with my cheek against my hand, and my hand propped up on my knee, trying not to miss a single word.

"Who are you? From what family? You haven't told me."

"I'm related to Madame Sabbagha. Her mother is my father's mother's sister."

"You're a liar. What do you want from me? Get up, my son. You're like my son. I can't anymore. Next thing you know you'll become senile like the Reverend, and I'll have to take care of you, and I can't anymore. But you're a young man. Honestly, my son, who are you, from what family?"

I told her I had nothing to do with the whole story, that I just wanted to listen, that Simaan Fayyad was our neighbor on "Little Mountain" and I'd known him for a long time. I knew him as a middle-aged man living with his sister in a small house in the Shalfoon area. I didn't realize he was the grandson of Fayyad Fayyad, the one who met with the czar's brother and covered the ground with salt and candles.

"You're a liar. Why are you lying to me?"

I stopped talking and so did she. She poured herself a glass of arak, didn't mix it with water, and slugged it down in one gulp.

"What do you do for a living?"

"I write. I work as a writer."

"What the hell is writing for, for God's sake?"

"To compose books and create heroes, so people can read them and enjoy them."

"Why don't they just watch TV? Wouldn't that be better?"

"Maybe. How should I know," I said to her to bring the subject to an end.

She looked up at the ceiling as if she were trying to remember something. Then she looked at me.

"I know a writer. We were working for Shaheen. Do you remember Shaheen? Of course you don't, you still hadn't broken out of the shell yet. There was a guy there who'd come every night. They said he was a writer, that he was like Gibran Kahlil Gibran. He was stuck on that blond German woman who socked him for his spirit and his money. God, she was a whore, how can anyone do that to a man she's in love with? But she was a whore. What can I tell you? He'd come every day, sit down, and wouldn't move for anything. And every night he'd bring her to his table and open a bottle. He was fat, with a face as white as a corpse. At the end of the night it'd turn out he didn't have any money. He'd take a beating and sit out on the sidewalk and throw up. They said he was a writer. Writer, my foot. I hope you're not like him."

"I am like him," I answered her.

"No, my son. You come from a good family. But what do you want with me?"

"I want to write about you."

"You're a liar, like Zaylaa. Nothing you say is true, you're full of lies. Honestly, what do you want with me? What can I help you with?"

"I want you to tell me stories."

"Why should I?"

"So I can write."

"Okay. Instead of telling you, why don't I just write them?"

She laughed out loud.

"My son, get up. Get out of here. Go, get out of here, say hello to your mother for me. It better not've been Zaylaa who sent you. He wants to get rid of me. The son of a bitch said he doesn't want me to sell flowers inside the Montana anymore. He says I'm bothering the customers. What kind of customers are they? Products of test tubes.

See what's happened? But there's nothing wrong with working for a living."

"You're right," I said to her.

"What do you mean, I'm right? It's as if you didn't understand a thing, like a deaf man at a wedding. My son, that's not the story. What's confusing me is why he's still around. They all died, or left, the ships were filled to capacity with people, but he's still around. Gandhi died, and he's still here. He killed his sister and maybe his mother. He became a ringleader, a big boss. The Jews came, and he's still here. Can you explain that to me? And now he wants to put me out of work, and I'll die and he'll still be around. Can you explain it to me? But you, what do you know. What did you say you do for a living, my son?"

She laid down on her bed, closed her eyes, and fell asleep. I got up to leave the room. She was lying on her left side, her legs curled up to her chest in a ball.

I stood there hesitantly, taken by a strong desire to shake her, to grab a hold of her and shake her. I approached her and she opened her eyes halfway and smiled.

"You're like my son. I'll get up in a minute. Let me rest for five minutes and then I'll get up."

I left her there and went. That was the last time I met with her, for four days later things exploded in Beirut. The uprising of February 6 took place, the Marines fled, and the war broke out again. The area where the Salonica Hotel was became a war zone, and Alice was lost.

When the bombing quieted in March of 1984, I went to the hotel and didn't find anyone. I found a huge barricade in front of the hotel and a group of armed men. I didn't dare ask them about the hotel owner or Alice. I went back home and I lost her. I decided to go to the nursing home to look for the Reverend Amin, perhaps he'd know something, or maybe I'd find her there, spending her last days in his company.

When Alice told me, she took me on a journey deep inside a black cave. "Memories are degrading," she said to me. Memories are a cave, I discovered while I was with her during those long years that her body shortened and changed into disconnected moments. Now, when I try to tell the story, I find that words are no longer signs that point the way but instead make me get lost, as if every word were tantamount to an assassination. How can I tell the story of a life never lived by its characters, a life that passed by them, like an act of will that pierced through them? That's how Alice and Gandhi lived; even Zaylaa was nothing more than a conduit for this act that pierces the body and changes it into masses of scattered cells.

I tell about Alice because I try to recall her to my memory, and so discover that memories are not degrading but rather a collection of illusions that can't be tied together, a chain that broke to pieces and sank to the bottom of the sea.

And Alice didn't cry anymore.

She cried only once. Then the tears that rolled from her eyes ceased to resemble crying. The tears became tears, while the weeping that shook her whole being, like a tree shaking in the wind, that weeping was gone when Abu Jamil cut the silver bracelet she brought with her from her father's house in Shekka. After that incident Alice bought lots of bracelets and sold them. She'd didn't care how many she bought and sold. Abu Jamil threw the two pieces out the window. He leaned over and picked them up from the floor, he picked up the two halves of the bracelet, threw them out the window, and took Alice to the nightclub. There life began to waste away like some intangible darkness. In the impending breakdown of light and darkness, Alice experienced the kind of love that chills your spine, and life that murders love and turns it into tattered rags. After Lieutenant Tannous al-Zaim left her, she discovered how a woman can get lost, like she did between Mosul and Aleppo. In Mosul, she lived those black nights that made her think of men as black clothes. In the black room Alice forgot the taste of Lieutenant Tannous, she forgot how his face radiated with desire and grief. In that room she felt she was dying, that death would come when it would come, in the image of a dark man, and so she surrendered to him and slept next to him without dreaming. In Aleppo she danced in a nightclub whose name she's forgotten. There were lots of Armenians there. She sang to them and they cried to the rhythm of her voice. Alice never sang in Beirut. She never did anything. She'd dance one or two numbers a night, but her job was to sit with the customers. In Aleppo she sang. The short nightclub owner who reeked of shish kebab came over and asked her to sing. She sang the popular song "My Love for You, Laura, Has Inflamed My Heart." A middle-aged man claiming he was from Antakya in the Iskenderun Province accompanied her on the oud. He bent over his oud as if he were about to fall over, and Alice sang, and the people cried. After she returned to Beirut, she started singing "My Love for You, Laura, Has Inflamed My Heart," but no one cried. Beirut never cried. Beirut was a city of sparkling nights that trotted across the surface of the sea. As she left Shaheen's, Alice would actually see the night walking on the water.

Saint George Hotel was plunged into the sea, the water around it breaking into patches of darkness and light.

It was true she lived alone, but her aloneness was not merely a series of spaces in her memory.

The second love of her life wasn't anything like the first. His name was Abu Abbas al-Yateem.

Abu Abbas al-Yateem would sit all day long on the fishermen's bench in the port of Ayn Mraysi wearing shorts and a short-sleeved shirt, summer and winter alike. He never changed, as if he were immune to the cold. He knew everyone. "They're all my friends," he said to Alice. He told her he didn't have a job; he used to be a fisherman, but now he was nothing. He'd sit and work would come to him. He'd sit because he didn't like work, and so work came to him on its own. Alice didn't like him at first. He came several times to Shaheen's and sat in the back waiting for her. When she'd finish with the other customers, she'd find him standing in front of her. "Hey, gorgeous. Let's get out of here," he'd say to her. Alice wouldn't go with him; she'd look at him as though she didn't see him and walk away. Every day she'd be greeted with the same old "Let's get out of here," but after a week, or a month, she couldn't remember exactly, and that wasn't important at any rate, she found herself with him.

Alice said when she was with him, she wasn't really with him. He had small eyes like two lentil beans, a wide forehead, hands like two big slabs of concrete. He'd take her to his room and sit her down outside next to the bench. He'd put a basket of fruit in front of her and talk. Alice would be shivering from the cold that penetrated her bones, but he'd just sit there, motionless, as if he didn't feel the cold at all. Then he'd take her behind the room, to a small courtyard filled with candles, and there he'd start flirting with her. The courtyard was fenced in, and the half-melted candles were all over the place, and there was the stench of urine and decay. There he'd make love to her standing up, and she wouldn't resist him. She'd just let him go back and forth and sway like a shadow rippling in the pale lights of dawn that resembled eggplant. Then they'd go to his room and sleep.

Alice said she didn't love him.

"Love comes later, at the end of the story. You know whether you're in love or not at the end. In the middle of the story, you're lost. Now I know. Tannous was all right, but this guy, al-Yateem, no. I didn't love him. It was something else."

That something else was the sea. Alice said he reminded her of the sea. He smelled like the sea. It was he who told her the sea was night. He'd swim in night's sea; he'd take off his shirt and jump in, and she'd watch how he'd get lost in night's sea. She'd stand behind the fence covered with candles and look to the sea, and she'd see night. Then when he'd come out of the water and salt, he'd make love to her again and leave her invigorated with water and unfulfilled desire.

During the day, she'd see him, surrounded by tourists and curious onlookers. He'd go to his room and get out an old notebook full of writing. He'd say the whole history of Ayn Mraysi was in that book. He'd stand in front of the cameras, pointing out to the journalists and foreigners the half-melted candles. He never tired of telling the story of the Italian nun.

The nun, he said.

The ship was sinking in the middle of the sea, he'd say, pointing to the distant horizon while people strained their eyes to see the point in the round, blue expanse. The ship sank and the nun came out of it, all by herself, everybody saw her, they saw her precious white headdress as it floated on the surface of the water. It floated as if it were a white box, and then the nun appeared. She wasn't swimming, she was walking, I swear to God she was walking, an Italian nun walking on the water. The white headdress rose up and the nun appeared in her torn clothes, while people stood right here, and he'd point to where the candles were, the people right here, and the nun coming from there, from that distant point, as though she were walking. "I," Abu Abbas said, "was a little boy, my father saw her, I swear on his grave, my father said she walked, and when she reached here, to the shore, people started running, one of them brought a white sheet, she wrapped herself in it and the sheet stuck to her body. She stayed here, she didn't ask for anything. She sat right here, there was no fence here, it was all sand and cactus, she knelt by the cactus and started praying. Then she built a little hut for herself and lived among the people, she was like a ghost. People said she was educated, God only knows. She'd go up there to drink, to the spring that was there, and he'd point with his hand to no place, and no one would ask him what happened to the spring, or where it was exactly, and there she built a school, she taught the children and she memorized the Qur'an, and her name became al-Raysi, mother superior, and the name of the area changed to Ayn al-Raysi, the spring of al-Raysi, and then, through mispronunciations and time, changed to Ayn Mraysi."

All this was written in the book. This is it, the book I inherited from my father, you can read it yourself. He'd put the book away and stand in front of the candles and smile.

And these candles, you forgot the candles, he'd say. These were from votive offerings, until now, people come and light candles for al-Raysi, who died here, and was buried here. Most of the people who come here are women, they get down on their knees and pray to al-Raysi and light candles, and she grants them what they pray for.

Abu Abbas told his story every day, and Alice never believed a word of it.

"You're a world-class swindler," she said to him.

"I'm a swindler, that's what they want. They want information. Ever since this became a bar area there's been a need for a history, they all want to know the history. What is history? Miracles and strange happenings, since the time of Saint Adam, peace be upon his soul, history is miracles and strange events."

"But you're lying to them."

"If I lie, they believe me, and if I don't lie, they don't believe me. But I don't lie; I say what I've heard, and what I've heard is true, because I heard it, right?"

"Of course not. Tell me, what was the nun's name?" Alice asked.

"Al-Raysi, everyone knows that."

"Right," said Alice.

Abu Abbas made a living from the story of al-Raysi, and, people said, from dealing hashish. Once he told Alice he was always out to make easy money. "The only way to make easy money is with hashish."

Alice didn't love him. She'd go with him almost every day, she'd give him money, but she didn't love him. Then, when he stopped coming to Shaheen's nightclub, she didn't feel anything at all, as if he never existed, she said. Alice didn't remember the candles of al-Raysi, except when al-Askary was killed. That day she ran to the fence and kneeled in front of the candles, lit a candle and cried. She prayed with all her heart for al-Askary not to die and made a vow to the Italian nun. She saw him before her, dead, but she didn't believe al-Askary could die. She lit three candles and cried, and when she went out from behind the fence she saw Abu Abbas. He pointed to her with his hand from the distance as if he didn't recognize her. She nodded her head to him. She nodded her head and worried the precious white headdress would fall. She walked slowly, as if the white sheet were glued to her body and prevented her from moving.

Zaylaa was different, Alice said. He was nothing like al-Askary. "Al-Askary was the biggest barhopper in town, what a guy."

When she described him, she became lost in a fog emanating from her eyes, she drowned in tears that wouldn't fall, tears that surrounded her face like a halo of water. Alice didn't expect to die. It was 1974, and Alice was staggering on her journey, and was almost collapsing under life's blows. She was forty-seven, lived alone in her room in Ayn Mraysi, and worked at the Blow Up nightclub. There she found only al-Askary. The bar owner told her she was getting old and should retire, so she went to Kamal al-Askary and told him. He had a lot of influence. A young, dark man, tall, broad shoulders, eyebrows so thin they looked like they'd been drawn with a pencil, he walked giving the impression that his legs moved by themselves and his body followed. He was the king. He'd go to all the bars, drink whatever he wanted, all the girls were at his beck and call, and he never paid. The beginning of every month he collected from everyone. No one complained. He protected the poor and helped them out, and he'd say he never touched alcohol, even though he drank a lot and never got drunk.

If it hadn't been for al-Askary, Alice would've found herself out on the streets. He was the one who told the bar owner that Alice should stay, and so she stayed. It's true things were topsy-turvy then, but she kept her job. The big upheaval was during the early seventies. Everything changed. Even people's tastes changed, as if they'd gotten tired of girls with plump bodies. Alice wasn't fat, she had a full figure, she "filled your eyes," as she put it. All of a sudden, everything changed. Kamal al-Askary died, and Alice was left all alone.

"That guy Zaylaa was a nobody, just a nouveau riche. The nouveaux riches are all dogs, because no one knows anything about them. I never liked him, nothing ever happened between us. Well, actually, once I was drunk and got crazy, he was crazy, too. He hit me and screamed and broke my bones. He was crazy. Then he started ramming his head against the wall and crying. The whole thing ended with crying, and I was watching. He refused to leave. He was crying so hard I thought he'd die from crying. I've never seen a man cry that way. Lieutenant Tannous, when he became like a woman, he got all screwed up and was ready to tear his hair out, but he didn't cry. Abu Jamil didn't cry when the owner of the Blow Up kicked him out and spat in his face because he was taking extra commission from the girls and selling them cocaine cut with impurities. But that guy Zaylaa, I don't what he was. He called himself a man, people like that aren't men, they're garbage."

And Kamal al-Askary died.

That day the Blow Up looked like a different place. Even now, no one knows, was al-Askary killed by Asad Awwad's bullet, or someone else's? Alice didn't know, no one who was there knew. All of a sudden the shooting started. They said the two of them were arguing over a girl. Al-Askary came into the nightclub and saw Awwad sitting with Rita, the Italian girl, and Rita was al-Askary's girl. Everyone knew Rita was al-Askary's girl. He came in and saw Awwad sitting with her with his arm around her, having a drink with her. Al-Askary didn't say anything. He stood up very quietly and then a shot was heard. Alice didn't know how it happened. Perhaps al-Askary wanted to teach Awwad a lesson, the way he taught the rest. Al-Askary's lesson was simple; he'd fire one shot at the bottle of whiskey and let the other guy know this was his territory. The other guy would back off and the problem would be solved.

Alice said all the officers in town were afraid of Kamal al-Askary; no one messed with him. Even Awwad knew how to play the game, because he was a professional. That's why no one could understand what happened, who, what, where, how. They said al-Askary drew his gun and fired at the very moment Awwad turned to fire, and they died together. Alice didn't believe it. She refused to believe al-Askary could die.

"Not Kamal al-Askary, no way. No one had a faster trigger finger than him."

Some of those who were there said al-Askary killed Awwad and then one of them shot him and he died. Others said al-Askary drew his gun but didn't fire, someone in the bar shot and killed both of them. They said it was murder, that the Second Bureau wanted to get rid of both of them. But Alice didn't believe that. They both fired and both died, that'd be better, she said, trying to tell the story from the beginning.

That day Beirut went up in flames.

Alice said the whole war started in the Blow Up. "If you'd seen it, if you'd been here, it was unbelievable, all of Beirut came out into the streets, the streets actually walked. Al-Askary was being carried over everyone's head, like he was flying and everyone else was below him. He was above everyone, and when he went down into the grave, the stories started. Women, if you'd seen the women. Women came and started crying. Veiled, unveiled, all sorts of women. He had an entire tribe. That's a real man. They killed him, that's what I think. Impossible, al-Askary is the one who shoots, no one shoots him. But he was shot. I saw how he fell, he fell like a mountain, like a heavy door."

Alice refused to believe it. But they both died. They both fired and they both fell. And Rita took off. Rita, the Italian girl, knew the truth, but she disappeared. She left and took the secret with her. There were rumors she worked for the Second Bureau, and rumors she was an Israeli spy, no one really knew.

That day Beirut lived through two funeral processions. One that crossed Corniche al-Mazraa in West Beirut and ended up at the Cemetery of the Martyrs, and one that walked from Abu Arbeed's gas station in East Beirut, passed by a gas station belonging to Asad Awwad, and ended up in Saint Mitr Cemetery.

Ever since that day, Beirut has been shrouded in night.

Alice said the civil war started there, and from that day not one day has passed like the previous ones.

"Everything went to pot," she said. "Women were treated like old shoes, and old shoes got to be more important than men, all the bullies left, and along came Zaylaa, and after him the midget, and after the midget, the Egyptian, none of them are men."

Alice said when Suad disappeared in 1976, she went to Zaylaa. The Montana was filled with the smell of those lights. Those dim lights placed in the corners would smoke like snuffed-out candles, and gave off a horrible smell. The place was filled with military-style uniforms, men sitting with women who looked like boys, and the fake laughter crackled through the place, while Zaylaa sat at the entrance like a rooster.

Gandhi came in. At first Alice didn't see him. He was wearing a broad-shouldered black jacket, walking with his head bent forward as if he would fall, and Alice was sitting alone at the bar, a glass of tea with some ice in front of her, a cigarette burning in the ashtray, and her eyes staring blankly, not seeing anything. Alice said she could sit like that for hours without thinking about anything. She'd sit there like a rock, eyes wide open, seeing nothing and hearing nothing. Gandhi looked for her amidst the shoes flying off of the customers' feet, big shoes in need of lots of shoe polish. He came up to the bar and stretched his hand out to Alice.

"Sit. What'll you have?" said Alice.

"No, I can't. I need you. It's urgent," Gandhi answered.

"Is everything all right?" she asked.

"The girl," he said.

"All the girls are at your service. Now you want girls?"

"No, no. My daughter Suad, Suad is missing, she disappeared two days ago, I looked everywhere, maybe they kidnapped her, maybe they killed her."

Gandhi's voice was faint and cracking with sadness.

"No problem," Alice said. "We'll talk to Zaylaa."

She took him to the door. Zaylaa was smoking greedily, as if he were chewing the smoke in his mouth before blowing it out of his wide nostrils. He listened to the story of Suad's disappearance without much concern.

"The crazy girl, aren't you talking about the crazy girl?"

"Yes. My daughter is sick."

"Yes, yes, I understand, we'll see what we can do, you go home, and sleep tight, I'll take care of it, don't worry. Hey, we're neighbors, aren't we? The Prophet enjoined us to be good to our neighbors."

"But how?" Gandhi asked.

"What do you mean, How? I told you I'd take care of it, that means I'll take care of it. You want the girl, don't you?"

Gandhi nodded his head politely.

"Okay. Go, the rest is up to me, go and sleep and tomorrow, God willing, you'll have your daughter."

Gandhi went to his house and slept, and Zaylaa kept sitting where he was. Alice wanted to go with Gandhi, but Zaylaa wouldn't let her.

"You get inside and take care of business. You think you're running your own business here?"

Alice went inside and Zaylaa didn't move from his spot. Actually, he came in at two in the morning and started drinking. Alice didn't dare ask him anything, for he had a reputation for beating up girls. All the girls were scared of him because he'd beat them up. She waited for him to tell her, but he didn't. She asked him in a soft voice. He laughed and asked her to come home with him. She went. It was a big house full of mirrors. The electricity was out. He lit a candle and asked her to massage his back for him. He took off his clothes, laid down on his stomach on his big bed, and she began massaging him. He asked her to take off her clothes; she took off her clothes. She took some cream and massaged his back. Then she heard him snoring, so she left him and went to another room and fell into a sound sleep.

The next day, around four in the afternoon, Alice passed Faysal's Restaurant and saw Little Gandhi sitting on a chair next to the newsstand.

He told her his daughter was back, and he was going to buy a present to take that evening to Zaylaa. He said he was going to buy him a pipe.

Alice tried to tell him Zaylaa didn't do anything, that he had nothing to do with his daughter's return.

Gandhi was set on buying the pipe and told her to come by in the evening before going to work so they could go together.

Suad came back.

Gandhi was sitting in his usual spot, his wooden box beside him, newspapers stacked around him, alongside the newspaperman who slept all day. He saw his wife coming to say the girl had come back, their daughter was home, so he ran off in a hurry.

At home he saw his daughter. She'd just come out of the shower, her long, black, curly hair spread out on her back. Her eyes had gotten bigger, more creases around them, and she was thin as a pole, trembling. She sat down next to her father, hugged him, and fell into a long crying spell and told him.

She said she went to their old house in Nabaa. She said she didn't find the house. She said they arrested her and took her to a shack. She said one of them started beating his head against the wall. She said they let her go, they put her on a truck, and in front of Salomi Circle one of them threw her on a garbage heap. She said she stayed on top of the heap all night, that she was afraid of the rats. She said a man came in the morning, and when he saw her he ran and started to scream. She said she got up from the pile of trash and ran, she said no one stopped her, she walked from Sin al-Fil to Hamra. She said she lost one of her shoes, so she walked half-barefoot. She said she wanted to sleep. She stopped talking.

Gandhi tried to get her to explain, but he couldn't understand anything.

His wife, who stood there listening to the girl without opening her mouth, yelled at her husband.

"The girl's finished. Your daughter's a lost cause, man, get on with your work, go."

Gandhi couldn't get up on his feet. He looked around, scared. He glanced back and forth from his wife to his daughter, cleared his throat, and didn't say anything.

He stood up and told his daughter to get dressed. She didn't move. Her mother stood her up, dressed her in her long blue dress, and Gandhi held her hand and took her to the hospital, to Doctor Atef's clinic. It was full of people. Gandhi sat his daughter down and approached the nurse. She looked at him as if she didn't know him.

"Please."

"Do you have an appointment?" she asked him.

"No."

"Sorry. Write your name and take an appointment, right now it's impossible, the doctor is all booked up."

"Please," Gandhi said in a somewhat hoarse voice. "I beg you, just tell the doctor, tell him Gandhi is dying, tell him and see."

"I'm sorry. The doctor only takes patients with appointments."

At this point Little Gandhi started screaming. No one had ever seen him scream before. This Little Gandhi had never raised his voice his entire life. Even when Spiro with the hat attacked him and hit him, he didn't open his mouth.

"The woman is a liar," he said. He took the blows to his face and walked away.

Gandhi didn't understand then what had happened, he was still a young man, working in that restaurant, waiting for Spiro with that woman while they occupied his bed and his attic room. Gandhi never came close to the woman. He'd stay downstairs, put up the tables and chairs, and mop. When Spiro attacked him and hit him, things got all mixed up for him.

He saw the woman coming downstairs. Spiro had left the restaurant after putting the black beret on his bald head. He opened the door and spit on the sidewalk, as he always did, and he saw the woman coming downstairs. He was leaning against the wall smoking a cigarette. The woman was wearing a see-through nightgown, her huge breasts swaying as she came down the stairs, and she was rubbing her eyes with her hands. He went up to her and held her breasts and heard the moans he listened to while waiting for them downstairs, mop in hand. Then he woke up. Before he woke up he saw everything had turned red. The woman was red, the floor was red, and he was red. Her sighs filled his ears and rang in them. He woke up to find himself sleeping on the chair, the lights still on in the store, the floor covered with water, and not a soul around.

The next day Spiro came and hit him. He didn't say why he was hitting him. He slapped him in the face and didn't go up to see his lady. Gandhi didn't scream or even open his mouth. He decided to leave the restaurant, and he did.

As for that day in the hospital, he shouted out loud, as if he were barking like a dog, and so Doctor Atef came running out.

"What's going on, Zeina?"

The nurse pointed to Gandhi.

"Please, Doctor, I beg you, I'm going to die."

"Come in, come in," the doctor said. "But stop shouting."

He grabbed his daughter and pushed her into the examining room. There were three women in there, so the doctor took Gandhi to a side room.

"Wait for me three minutes, three minutes, I'll be with you."

Gandhi waited, and Suad waited. The doctor took her into the examining room.

"What's the story?" the doctor asked.

"Examine her, please, she disappeared for three days, I beg you, I've lost my honor, my reputation, I want to know."

"Shut up," said the doctor.

He sat the girl in a chair and lifted her skirt over her thighs.

"Get out," the doctor said.

"No, I won't go, I want to see."

The doctor examined her for a few seconds, then looked at Gandhi.

"Congratulations, sir. Your honor and reputation are intact. She's still a virgin."

The girl didn't open her mouth; she was unconscious.

"Now tell me the story," Doctor Atef said.

Gandhi told him. "The medicine isn't available. She should take four pills every day, you know the situation, there's no medicine."

The doctor took the prescription and read "Sordinol." No problem, he said, wrote her a new prescription, and said she'd be all right, God willing.

She didn't get better. She'd take the pills and become lethargic, as if she'd been hypnotized. The only person she'd talk to was Abu Saeed al-Munla. He'd be sitting in front of his store and invite her to come drink some yogurt. He'd run to Malku's store and buy her a bottle, and say to her, "Blessed one." Suad would stand in front of his store a long time while he talked to her and waited for a sign. Abu Saeed al-Munla said he was waiting for a sign from that girl. "These are the ones, these are the ones." When Malku the Assyrian would ask him what he was talking about, Abu Saeed would say he doesn't understand, these are the ones God has blessed and taken to see what we don't see. We don't see, and Abu Saeed would give his theory about Beirut. Beirut is an island, he'd say. An island asleep in the sea, asleep atop a ferocious beast, and every seventy years the beast gets restless and the city is turned upside down, and the more it gets turned upside down, the closer it comes to the end. Seven times the beast turned over and so did the city. Now we're in its eighth topple. Abu Saeed said Mihran Efendi, the Turk, he was the one who told him these stories, when he was a child. Mihran Efendi was the only Turk who refused to leave Beirut after World War I. He was in love. He came by foot from the Suez Canal to Beirut, only to find that his sweetheart had gotten married. He stayed in Beirut and decided to wait for her, then he became a Beiruti himself. Beirut makes Beirutis out of everyone. Mihran Efendi, who became a shipping contractor, was the first to predict the disaster. He used to say Beirut was a sea animal—you love it the way you love animals. A city without a history, it turns upside down, its whole history is that it turns over on its belly and starts everything rolling along.

Abu Saeed was convinced. Mihran Efendi's stories were convincing. He remembered him sitting on the chair in their garden, his father welcoming him in Turkish, and the Turk telling stories about the First World War and how the Turks were defeated at the Suez Canal and were scattered in the wilderness, and how he alone escaped, crossing the Sinai Desert and Palestine to Lebanon, where he stayed and died and never married. Mihran Efendi died before the sea animal turned over and killed everyone.

When the animal turned over that morning, and Abu Saeed heard the bullets that ripped Sunbuk apart, he looked out from his balcony and saw Sunbuk kneeling down and Gandhi wrapped in newspapers. It was drizzling as he shouted, "Allahu Akbar!" That day, everyone remembered how the screams in the city rended the skies. That day, the blessed one was walking beside her mother, and both of them seemed like strangers in this world. They walked along and didn't stop to look at Little Gandhi's corpse. The color black covered everything. The city was black, and the boots of the Israeli soldiers were everywhere.

Fawziyya and her crazy daughter walked to Mashta Hasan, that's what Alice said. Alice said she thought the two women went there. As for Husn, no one saw him. Alice searched for him a long time, but he disappeared. Master Ahmad, the hair salon owner, told Alice he hadn't seen him since that morning. He said he used to sleep in the salon every night. Master Ahmad said he didn't go to work that morning, he'd been away for seven days, and when he came back he found the broken glass scattered everywhere, but he didn't find Husn.

Alice said Husn died, he went to war and died. Didn't you hear death? she said to me. All the young men went to their deaths. They'd fire the B7 missiles and shout "Allahu Akbar!" and die. That day everyone died. By myself I took him, I took Gandhi to the grave and came back to the hotel. They all died, al-Munla was shot and won't recover, the Assyrian said he was leaving, and Husn disappeared.

He had small hands, dry, pitch-black fingers. The hands and fingers were covered with interlocking black splotches, like pieces of skin stuck on top of one another. Little Gandhi wasn't bothered by the colors of his hands, he knew this was part of his trade, and that when he took up the shoe-shine box he'd chosen the world of shoe polish that colors shoes and hands and sidewalks. It was a plain wooden box, with a raised tongue for customers to put their shoes on, special compartments for the shoe polish containers, a shaving brush he used to wash the shoes with soap, a toothbrush for getting the sides of the shoes, two brushes for shining, and a thick black pad. Gandhi didn't choose this trade, it came to him as if it were waiting for him. After he left the restaurant, buying the box was all he could do. He went to a carpenter in Nabaa who specialized in making coffins and asked him to make him a box. He picked up the box and walked from Nabaa to Hamra Street. He sat in front of Jarjoura's Restaurant, then later changed to Faysal's. No one asked him why he was sitting there. The newspaper dealer Naeem Nassar welcomed him as if he'd been waiting for him. Naeem Nassar had been selling newspapers for twenty years, in that very spot. He'd lay out the papers and magazines on the sidewalk, paying close attention to the color scheme, sit down on a small chair in front of his stall, and smoke incessantly. He knew everything that went on, for he'd been selling newspapers since childhood, and so would his son after him. He'd read everything and advise the customers what to buy. Naeem Nassar welcomed Gandhi. At that time his name hadn't become Gandhi yet, he was Abd al-Karim. Abd al-Karim would sit behind his box as if he were stuck to it. He never lifted his head, even when he got paid for shining the shoes. As though he were an old man, Little Gandhi's soft beard looked like black splotches on his dark face, and he wore a dark suit summer and winter. He sat like a child or an old man, for this profession is suited only to children and old men. Gandhi didn't change the rules of the profession, for he was always leaning over the shoes like an old man, and when he carried his box to go back to his room in Nabaa, he ran like a child.

The Reverend Amin was the first to draw his attention to how dirty his hands were and suggested he wash them with kerosene. Gandhi didn't use kerosene. He let the shoe polish build up on his hands, to the point that when he polished, his hands looked like part of the shoe.

The shoes were endless. Gandhi could tell a man's personality from his shoes: worn-out shoes were a sign of carelessness, shoes that were always like new were a sign of fearfulness, shoes that weren't laced properly were a sign of sexual potency, shoes with the backs folded down like slippers were a sign of craziness. He'd go on about this with the American, Dr. John Davis, who was impressed with Gandhi's ability to polish shoes and sit for long hours bent over his hands without getting tired.

What really preoccupied Gandhi's mind was mirrors; he wanted to turn each shoe into a mirror. He especially loved black shoes, for brown shoes, no matter how much they shined, never became like mirrors. A black one, on the other hand, could really be polished and became like one solid piece. After the black shoe polish was poured on, it became one, as though it were cast in black, and with the first rub of the brush the shine would start and brighten it, the black color would be opened to the world, and Gandhi would see the parts of his face on the shoe's upper. The whole world enters shoes, and the man standing there, most often holding a newspaper, reading, doesn't understand the importance of what is taking place atop his shoes. Only Gandhi knew, he knew that everything, the buildings and the faces, and the underground water pipes, and the sidewalk, everything enters into shoes, transforming them into a new world being born.

Gandhi hated the two-toned shoes that came into style in the late fifties, white on the sides with blotches of brown in the middle. Dying white shoes was bothersome, because he didn't use the kind of polish that coated the leather; instead he had to use a water-soluble dye he got out of a long bottle, using some cottony material—a square white cloth upon which the white liquid was poured. Gandhi would put it on the shoe as if he were performing surgery. That was only for covering the shoe with the color; dying it was another thing altogether. Dying it would bring back the value of the shoe, not just cover it. White was for covering. Women's shoes with the sharp pointed toes were impossible, because the pointy tip made it difficult to round out the color, so the shoe would remain only covered with the color, even if it was black. The true work was in the black shoe, when you could actually smell the leather, the "chevreux" style, or the "box" style. Gandhi preferred the box even though the chevreux was softer. The box could truly be transformed into a mirror, and the city transformed into a shoe.

When Gandhi would finish with the shoes that were sent to him, he'd stand them up against the wall and use them to watch the reflection of people's feet as they walked by. When the customer would come to get his shoes, Gandhi would ask him to look carefully and see his face in them.

Once the Reverend Amin got upset. That was at the beginning of their long relationship. Gandhi asked him to look at the reflection of his face in his shoes, so the Reverend thought this short shoe shiner was making fun of him. He gave him a belittling look and left without paying.

He told Gandhi the next day he forgot to pay because he was so upset with him.

Gandhi refused to take any money and said he'd forget about the whole thing, that he wanted to prove to the Reverend that everything could be turned into a mirror. From that day on the Reverend Amin became Gandhi's friend, and was convinced that everything could be turned into a mirror.

He said to Madame Lillian that her eyes were the mirror of the world, and didn't ask her to fly. But she was a crazy woman, what can you ask of a crazy woman?

The Reverend Amin didn't know how he asked her to fly. He saw his voice coming out of him, thick and melodious, as if it weren't his voice.

"Fly. Fly."

And he started waving his hands like a fan.

He was engulfed with a strong desire to see her jump. When he stood her in front of the window after turning out the light, he stood behind her and started flapping like a fan. He opened the window and tried to push her, to make her fly. The woman got scared and threw herself onto the floor and started crying.

"Everything is a mirror," Amin said to Gandhi, watching him bent over his shoes, as if he wanted to swallow the world.

"And God is a mirror, God is a mirror but man refuses to see his face. God is his face, but man is afraid."

Madame Lillian got scared and started to cry. Gandhi told Fawziyya when he married her that he didn't like this profession. He liked to see shoes shimmering in the light, but he didn't like the profession, he'd rather leave it. When the dog came into the picture, he did leave it and opened his own restaurant.

Fawziyya wouldn't say anything, she'd agree without saying anything. She'd give birth to the babies and the babies would die. Husn came, and lived, and after him Suad, and then Fawziyya went back to death; the baby would be born dead or die shortly after birth.

Gandhi was dizzy with sadness. He took her to see every doctor at the American University, the ones he knew and the ones he didn't know. They gave her medicine and vitamins. He spent all his money on medicine. During his last visit to Dr. Naseeb Suleiman, the doctor advised Gandhi to stop the pregnancies. Fawziyya was sitting there with her head down while the doctor talked to Gandhi, telling him it wasn't good, that the woman could die. You have to stop the pregnancies.

Gandhi shook his head in agreement and told the doctor the best thing would be a divorce, because he'd tried everything he knew, but Fawziyya kept getting pregnant, he'd come near her and she'd get pregnant, and he couldn't take it anymore.

"Buy a kabbout,"[9] the doctor said.

"What for?" asked Gandhi.

"Buy a kabbout and sleep with her, and . . . you know."

"Of course I know," said Gandhi.

They went out of the doctor's office. Fawziyya went home, and Gandhi went to Souq Sursuq and bought a heavy wool coat. He went home and slept with Fawziyya.

When Gandhi told the story of the coat, he'd have tears in his eyes and he'd laugh. He'd put his hands over his

9. In colloquial Lebanese, *kabbout* means "coat," but it is also the word used for condom.

eyes and shake his head, as if he wanted to stop himself from laughing.

"I was stupid. The coat taught me to be sly, and if I weren't sly, how do you think I could survive? What kind of life is this, sitting and waiting around? Those who wait around will get nowhere, nowhere but the grave. But life is different. As I was saying, dear sir, I bought the wool coat and went home and slept with the woman with the coat on top of us. We were dripping with sweat. I was going to choke, and she was about to die. She'd be under me, saying over and over 'Oh God, Oh God, Oh God' and I'd be saying it along with her, and the sweat came down like rain. I said, it's okay, it's better than the woman dying. Then I find out she's pregnant. I paid six liras for that coat. Do you know how much six liras is? Like two thousand today, tomorrow it'll be worth a hundred thousand. What did I know. I paid and we drowned in sweat and she still got pregnant, and I went crazy."

"I went to see Dr. Naseeb and I told him. He laughed so hard his eyes watered, and kept laughing till he almost died. He was rolling on the floor with laughter, so I started laughing. If the doctor laughs, the patient should laugh, too, right? But I wasn't a patient."

Dr. Naseeb was ready to hear anything but that story. He went out of the clinic and called the rest of the doctors. They all laughed and Gandhi laughed with them. Then he felt like he was surrounded, like a cat surrounded by a bunch of mischievous children. He closed his eyes and started gasping for air. Dr. Naseeb noticed, and so he changed the subject. He started speaking in English. After everyone left and only Gandhi was left, the doctor said, "You go to the pharmacy, Heliopolis Pharmacy, and buy a kabbout from there."

He explained to him the virtues of the condom.

"That day I understood," Gandhi said. "Life is like the condom: you either use it, or become one yourself and others use you. I used to be one, but not anymore, now I'm sly. I went to the drugstore and bought six condoms for twenty-five piasters. But she wouldn't do it at first, then she went along, women go along with things, and she said it's in God's hands, and we left it in God's hands."

When Little Gandhi married his cousin Fawziyya, he knew nothing but trusting things to God. The story of his escape couldn't have happened without this faith in God. Everyone said the boy was dead. In Mashta Hasan they said the beast had killed him, but Husn, his father, knew he wasn't dead. He told his wives and daughters the boy wasn't dead. He called them together around his bed during his final moments alive and told them the boy wasn't dead. He said he saw him once in Beirut, and that Abd al-Karim gave him five liras to take a taxi back to the village, and that he wanted his son, that he didn't want to die. He started screaming that he didn't want to die, while Sheikh Zakariyya stood over his head, prompting him as he refused to repeat the words, then his lower jaw began to tremble, his voice faded, and Sheikh Zakariyya was saying, "Husn, son of Najibi, if the two angels have come to you, tell them God is my Lord, Muhammad is my patron, Islam is my religion until resurrection day." And Husn, the son of Abd al-Karim al-Ahmadi al-Mughayiri staggered under Sheikh Zakariyya's words, dying.

After the burial, Abd al-Karim came back to the village once, to get married. He married Fawziyya, the daughter of his uncle the lupine vendor. They sat him down, and they sat her down, he was wearing his new black suit, she was wearing a white gown, and people surrounded them, clapping. His father's second wife was squeezing lemons, preparing the lemonade and serving it. Fawziyya was sit-

ting on the round stone, and he sat facing her waiting for
Sheikh Zakariyya. The sheikh arrived, so everyone clapped
and the singing and dancing began. Then the sheikh raised
his hand and said to the bride, he asked her and she said,

"I am sitting on the stone, hear O divine Lord, I love
this man, according to the law of God and His Messenger."

He asked her to repeat, and so she repeated the sentence three times. Sheikh Zakariyya approached her and
placed a handful of wheat in her hand.

He turned to Abd al-Karim, and the little man said, "I
am sitting on the ground, hear O Lord of Lords, I love this
woman, according to the law of God and His Messenger."

He asked him to repeat, and so he repeated the sentence three times. Then he asked Fawziyya to stand, and so
she stood, and sprinkled the wheat over Abd al-Karim's
head and let out a single shrill.

Gandhi took her and they got in a taxi and went back
to Beirut. He didn't bathe, as was the custom, and he
didn't take her to his father's house, where the people
would wait to see the white sheet stained with blood. He
was like a stranger in his village. He accepted going
through the ceremony on the stone because the lupine vendor insisted on it. They wrote the marriage contract in
Beirut, and Gandhi wanted to marry her without going
back to the village, but the lupine vendor insisted.

"A marriage has to have a stone, my son. When a person dies, he puts his head on a stone, and when he gets
married, the woman sits on a stone, it can't be otherwise,
you can't have a marriage without a stone."

Gandhi agreed. He bought a mirror, two dresses, a
pair of shoes, and a broom and brought twenty kilos of
lemons with him to the village, and ten kilos of sugar.
When it was all over, he took Fawziyya to the little house

in Nabaa, which would later become a restaurant. That was 1938; Nabaa was all dirt roads and there was no water and no electricity. Fawziyya had difficulty at first. She said she hated Armenians, then she started liking them and got used to everything. When Gandhi left Nabaa early in 1976, escaping the bombs and the war, he lived on the ground floor of the Burj al-Salam building on Hamra Street. The only thing Fawziyya grieved over was Nabaa. She said she hated Hamra Street and felt she was living in a cage.

"You're talking as if that is the reason," Gandhi said to her. "If you hadn't talked that way, the girl wouldn't have run away."

"She ran away because there's no more medicine, you know that," his wife said.

When the girl came back, and Gandhi discovered she was still a virgin, he felt he'd tried everything. Her running away was his last chance. He'd done everything, but she didn't get better. She'd lost so much weight she'd become thin as a pole, and she didn't talk.

How did Suad's sickness all start?

Gandhi didn't know, and Fawziyya didn't know. Gandhi didn't remember his daughter complaining of anything. She was like any other little girl. When Gandhi would try to remember her childhood as the doctor asked, he drew a blank.

"I swear I don't remember, Doctor. Yes I do. She went to school, but I took her out because she's a girl, she was twelve years old and I figured that was enough. I put her with Um Jamil the seamstress, and she learned to sew and cut patterns, she was so good, she knew how to do everything perfectly."

"And then?" the doctor would ask.

159

"And then, then what? There is no then, doctor. I mean, she got like this."

"What do you mean like this?" the doctor would ask.

"She'd brood over things, and wouldn't eat, not one night passed when I'd wake up and find her asleep, she'd be sitting up in her bed, with her eyes wide open, as if she were seeing things we couldn't see."

"And what would she say?"

"Who?" asked Gandhi.

"Her. What would she say?" the doctor said.

"I'd sit next to her. I'd wake up in the middle of the night and find she wasn't asleep. I'd sit next to her and talk to her, and I wouldn't understand. She'd speak, but as if I weren't understanding, as if she weren't talking to me, as if she were talking to someone else."

"And before that?" the doctor would ask.

"There is no before," Gandhi would answer. "She knew she was sick, sometimes she'd tell me she was sick, and then I'd think everything was all right, but she'd go back."

"Could it've been the war?" the doctor would ask.

Gandhi would try to remember. Nothing had happened, the war was everywhere, his daughter before the war, before April 13, 1975, and before the siege of Nabaa, before people were kicked out of their homes and degraded. Gandhi wasn't kicked out of his home, and wasn't degraded. He told Fawziyya he understood what was going on. He told her they were going to drive out the Palestinians and the Muslims and kill them. He told her to go with him. He took her and the two children and went to Ras Beirut, and there he found a small room in Witwat Quarter. Then he moved to the ground floor of the building, thanks to Zaylaa, and stayed there. He didn't live the degradation and the expulsion from his home. Gandhi knew about it, he found out about it, and fled with a trick. He paid the Armenian and told him he wanted to go to West Beirut. The Armenian didn't go with them. His daughter Navir took them to West Beirut. She drove the car, and my God, Navir was snow white, white as a sheet. She came early in the morning and told them to follow her. They followed her to the car, and she wouldn't let them take anything.

"Everything on the ground. We can't take anything with us," Navir said.

Gandhi left everything but his wooden box. She tried to stop him. He left the mirror and the broom and the mattress and the rest of the dowry.

"Not the box," Gandhi said. "No way, it's my livelihood."

She let them get into the car, Gandhi next to her with the box in his hands, and Fawziyya and Suad and Husn in the backseat in the big black Chevy. She didn't stop at any of the checkpoints. When the checkpoint guards saw Navir, they opened the way for her as if she were godsent. Suad sat next to her mother in a stupor, as if she weren't seeing or hearing at all.

Suad was like that, didn't see or hear at all.

Gandhi tried to tell her story to the doctor, but he remembered that doctors laugh at people. He remembered the kabbout doctor and the pharmacist. He told Alice he went to the pharmacist at Heliopolis Pharmacy and bought condoms for twenty-five piasters, as the doctor had told him. Gandhi held the package and asked the pharmacist how to use them. The old man bared his teeth and told him, using his finger in a disgusting way to show where it went. He opened the package, took a condom and inflated it, and told Gandhi to take it. Gandhi held it and then threw it onto the floor and left the pharmacy with the man's laughter ringing in his ears.

Gandhi couldn't solve the problem, after the doctors failed and the girl became like an idiot who didn't have any idea what was happening around her. Gandhi agreed to Fawziyya's suggestion. He took her to the village and there he met with Sheikh Zakariyya, a different Sheikh Zakariyya than the one who married them and buried his father. He was related to the first Zakariyya and looked just like him; the little cough, the thick fingers, the white eyebrows. After he put his hand on the girl's head Sheikh Zakariyya said, "There is no power and no strength save in God Almighty. I can't do anything, my son, the girl is possessed by an evil spirit. I can't."

He advised him to take her to Sheikh Hasan al-Alwani in the city of Hama. Gandhi went to a friend's place in Hums and she helped him get a taxi to Hama to meet with Sheikh Hasan al-Alwani. If you didn't know Sheikh Hasan al-Alwani, you didn't know anything. He was one of a kind. "My God, he was one of a kind," Gandhi said. "How beautiful, meekness, a melodious voice, a quiet social gathering, and prayer." When you visited him you'd think you were going to the next world, and he'd be sitting there. He sat in the front of the hall, three fireplaces around him burning red wood, and there were men, women, and prayers. When Gandhi entered with Suad, they heard a voice ordering them to kneel, so they kneeled. Gandhi tried to stand up after his knees started to get numb, but he heard the same command, so he kneeled again. They kneeled for about an hour, and there were lots of other people kneeling around them. Sheikh Hasan al-Alwani sat motionless, as if he were a stone.

Abd al-Karim heard the order to approach. He heard the voice say, "Abd al-Karim son of Husn son of Abd al-

Karim." But he hadn't given his name to anyone yet. He went in to see the sheikh with everyone else, and kneeled like they did, and didn't tell anyone his name or what he wanted. When he entered, someone covered the girl's head.

Abd al-Karim got up when he heard his voice, took his daughter's hand, and went forth.

"No, no. Suad stays there," the voice said.

He brought his daughter back to her place and ordered her to kneel. She didn't say anything, she knelt as she had before, and Gandhi went forward.

"Take these," the voice said, and he gave him three papers, sealed with a waxlike substance.

"The first paper is for the dog to eat," the voice said.

"Yes," Gandhi answered.

"Don't speak. Be quiet," someone said.

"The second paper you place on a forsaken grave."

Gandhi bowed his head and didn't speak.

"The third paper you boil in hot water and give it to your daughter to drink, and she will be healed, God willing."

Gandhi tried to get close to Sheikh Hasan al-Alwani to kiss his hand, but a man standing next to the sheikh stopped him and ordered him to take his daughter and leave. Outside he paid twenty liras and went on his way.

He took the three papers and did what he was told to do. He fed the first one to the dog after mixing it with some meat, and placed the second on an abandoned grave in Beirut, and boiled the third and gave the water to Suad to drink. But Suad was not healed. Gandhi was sure she was healed, but she wasn't. She went back to the way she was and worse. She started getting out of her bed at night, walking around and talking deliriously, saying things no one could understand, as if she wanted to kill herself. One of those nights she tried to kill her mother. Gandhi woke up to the sound of Fawziyya screaming and saw his daughter standing in front of her mother's bed. Fawziyya was screaming and said Suad tried to strangle her. After that Gandhi was lost, he no longer knew anything. Abu Saeed al-Munla was the one who told him about Sheikh Tayyar.

Gandhi took his daughter and went to Tartous. There he found Sheikh Tayyar sitting in a black room near the seacoast. Sheikh Tayyar was all alone, no fireplaces, no fire, nothing. Gandhi and his daughter entered and sat down on some cushions on the floor. The sheikh was sitting on a chair; a set of white worry beads that resembled his thin white beard dangled from his hand.

Sheikh Tayyar asked Little Gandhi to tell him his story. He listened and asked about small details the little man didn't know about. He asked a lot about the girl's birth, about her eyes when she was born — were they open or closed? Gandhi didn't know. He gave rough answers, and said he didn't know exactly, and suggested to the sheikh that he bring his wife.

"It's not necessary, not necessary, I know," the sheikh said.

He looked at the girl's wandering eyes and asked Gandhi, "Does she mention him?"

"Who, Master?" asked Gandhi.

"The king," the sheikh said. "Does she talk about the king or mention names you don't know?"

"No," Gandhi said. "I don't think so. I've never heard her mention the king."

"Then it's nothing to worry about," the sheikh said in a quiet voice. "Nothing to worry about, there's no evil in the girl, she needs blood. She must bleed, her blood must mix with a man's blood, a man must make her bleed. Marry her off, the first night she'll be cured, blood cures.

164

Get up, man, take your daughter and get her married, she'll be fine."

Gandhi got up and took his daughter to Beirut. Fawziyya was the one who recommended her cousin in Tripoli.

"We don't have anyone else, he's like my brother, he'll do it."

Gandhi went to Tripoli. He arrived in the city at night, so he didn't see anything, and didn't remember, and didn't feel any longing for Master Rashid's bakery, the one that looked like a key. He found his wife's cousin's house with no problem, it was in Bab al-Tibbaneh, above Arab Bakery. He got to the bakery, went up to the third floor, and knocked on the door. Gandhi had never seen the man who was to become his son-in-law but once, but, as Fawziyya said, "Need justifies the forbidden." He knocked on the door with a bitter taste in his mouth.

"Is this the residence of Hasan al-Bakkar?" Gandhi asked the woman who had cracked the door open for him.

"Please come in," the woman said and opened the door.

He went in, and Hasan al-Bakkar, who was sitting with his eight children around him having dinner, gave him a hug. They invited him to eat with them, so he extended his hand and ate one bite.

Hasan al-Bakkar showed his surprise at this unexpected visit.

"Is everything all right, cousin?" he asked.

"Everything is fine," Gandhi said. "There's nothing wrong. I just came for a visit."

"Welcome, welcome," the man said, chewing his food.

After dinner the teacups made their rounds, the television was turned on, and the house was filled with noise.

Gandhi went close to Hasan al-Bakkar, and in a soft voice he told him the purpose of his visit.

"Get married, me?" the man said, raising his voice. His wife turned toward them with an alarmed expression on her face.

Gandhi explained to him it was a matter of formality. "Divorce her, Cousin, divorce her after two days, but this is what Sheikh Tayyar said to do."

"You want me to marry a crazy woman?"

"She's not crazy, Cousin, not crazy, this is a curse from God. The girl has to get better, take her without a dowry, without anything, and divorce her."

The man said he wouldn't do it, and his wife started screaming.

"They've followed us here, the women have followed me to my home."

There was lots of commotion and children screaming.

Gandhi got up. His wife's cousin didn't ask him to spend the night. He let him go at ten o'clock at night, in the cold, not knowing how he was going to get back to Beirut.

"He just let me leave his house and walk, the son of a bitch," Gandhi told his wife. "To hell with relatives, they're nothing but a bunch of scorpions, that's what my Aunt Khadija used to say, God rest her soul."

The girl didn't get married, and her condition got worse. Gandhi didn't tell all this to Doctor Naseeb, he only told him she didn't eat or sleep, and that she hallucinated, and when anyone visited, she'd sit on the edge of the bench and stare at them, and say she was sick. Gandhi told the doctor the girl spoke unintelligibly, and that he was afraid she'd get lost in the streets.

The doctor explained to him that the girl's condition was complicated, and prescribed some medicine for her.

He said she was suffering from a nervous disorder called "schizophrenia," or a split mind.

"What does split mind mean?" Gandhi asked.

"It's a mental illness, and she can get better, give her the medicine."

"You mean, she's split in half, she sees double?" Gandhi asked.

The doctor laughed. "No, no. It's a kind of depression, a deep sadness, sometimes people get lost and then they come back."

At the time Gandhi was afraid. He was afraid of split minds and became afraid of Suad. He'd see her split in two. He started seeing everything separated. When she came back home, after she ran away to Nabaa, she came back without having bled, and without dying. He told the doctor she became emaciated because the medicine wasn't available. He knew she went looking for her blood, and that her blood came back to her, and that there was no hope.

This city is like that, a split city. Everything in it fell apart, just as Kawkab al-Sharq did.

Gandhi was listening to Zaylaa as he told about how he would kill people. "A man who doesn't kill is not a man," Zaylaa said.

Gandhi would tell Alice he wasn't a man, because he didn't like killing, "But maybe I killed him."

"You?" Alice laughed. "You kill?"

"Yes, me, but I'm not sure."

Gandhi didn't know. When that man he was talking about was killed, Gandhi didn't know, but he was there. Gandhi was still a young man, twenty years old or so, working over his shoe-shine box. Every weekend he'd go to the horse races, bet his money again and again, and the horses wouldn't win. It was the sight of the horses that kept him going every week, and made him spend all the money he made during the week. These horses weren't like the ones at Abu Hurayra's tomb, where they would trample men, and where Gandhi would see legs and backs and listen to the screams of women. Here the screaming was different. Gandhi would scream, he'd scream and men he didn't know standing next to him would scream. He felt he was alone in front of the scene of the charging horses. He felt he could jump and do whatever he wanted.

At Elias al-Halabi's funeral, he trampled over the man and took off.

That was many years ago, but when Gandhi told the story to Dr. Davis, he said "last year." The tall American professor smiled and said it happened in 1935, around thirty years ago.

"Whatever," Gandhi said.

Gandhi was with everyone else, everyone went. That day the electric tram of Beirut went off the track. All of Beirut and the funeral procession were in Burj Square. People gathered on balconies and climbed the walls. Gandhi was on the balcony of Kawkab al-Sharq. And while the coffin floated over the heads, and Abdu al-Inkdar, and Saad al-Deen Shatila, and Ghandoor Zuraiq walked with their bamboo sticks under the coffin, and the funeral dirges filled the place, the balcony of Kawkab al-Sharq collapsed. The people were tiny, they looked like short scurrying bodies beneath a coffin the size of your hand. Everyone was running and screaming. Gandhi stood surrounded by a lot of people, among them Hasan al-Atrash, who sold betting tickets at the horse races. Hasan al-Atrash died. His head was squashed beneath the slab of concrete that fell. Gandhi shook with the ground and fell down. He said it felt as though things were spinning, as if he were falling into a deep valley. I stood up, he said he stood up and tried to run. People were on the ground, and the ground was on top of the people, and the coffin of Elias al-Halabi sped off as if it were running away.

I trampled over him. Gandhi said he trampled over a man. "I may have killed him, I don't know, maybe, I don't know. But I took off, I became a runaway, as if I were a criminal, running to I don't know where, I kept walking till I got home, and at home I slept, I put my head down on my pillow and went to sleep. And I never wanted to get up, I couldn't."

Gandhi told Alice he didn't know why he loved to sleep that much. In this world you can't open your eyes; if you do, everything starts spinning. Nothing has any taste to it.

Alice believed that things had a lasting flavor. She couldn't forget that things have a taste that stays in your mouth, even after they're gone.

When the Egyptian said to her that Beirut is like cardboard, her eyes smiled.

"You don't know anything, my friend. What do you mean, cardboard? The whole world is cardboard, but Beirut never slept, even now it doesn't sleep. Who can sleep in a place where there is no sleep? You're all sleepy because you're afraid, I'm not afraid, I don't sleep and I'm not afraid."

Zaylaa would look at her, trying to scare her, and Alice wasn't scared. She told him the real bullies were dead, and he, with his short hair like the American soldiers, didn't scare her.

"The bullies are gone, Ibn Zaylaa, you son of a bitch."

Ibn Zaylaa would let her get away with it, not because he was a son of a bitch, but because she was a poor soul.

What did this woman know about bullies? Before Zaylaa killed his sister by strangling her with his bare hands, he'd killed many others. Zaylaa was a soldier in the Lebanese army, then the war started and he became just like everyone else.

"When the war comes we fight," he said to Lieutenant Ahmad al-Hasan. "Sir, we need to live, we need to buy televisions, we need money, we need war."

Zaylaa went to war. The day he saw Captain Salah Aamer crying like a baby, he understood that the war would go on without those who philosophized and discussed the war of the people and the masses, those would die, and the war would go on without them. Zaylaa left these organizations and went where he should go. There wasn't one organization or group he didn't work for. He trafficked hashish and traded weapons and wound up in charge of the Montana Bar.

"I protect the bar. Without me, what would've happened to all of you?" he said to Alice.

"You're right, Zaylaa, without you we'd have become prostitutes, now we're respectable ladies, without you, someone else would've come along."

"I'm better than some, Madam."

"You're just like the others, you're not special, you are the others, ask me, I'll tell you, but you don't know how to talk and you don't know how to listen."

"Shut up! If you don't like it, leave."

"I don't like it, but I'll shut up. I'll shut up because the conversation is over, when the conversation is over I'm no longer the Alice who . . . "

"I know, I know," Zaylaa said. "Please, don't tell us about "The Leader" and Abd al-Karim Qasim and all that bullshit."

"What's there to tell?" Alice said to Gandhi.

Gandhi liked Hasan Zaylaa. "If it weren't for him, they'd have killed me," he said to her. Gandhi said they wanted to kill him because he lived in the cellar of Burj al-Salam. The cellar was empty when Gandhi fled from Nabaa and came to live in it. Some armed men came and told him to get out. And if it hadn't been for Zaylaa, he would've been killed.

"Zaylaa is a good man, but he's temperamental. He gets drunk and says whatever come to his mind, but he has a good heart."

"Right," Alice said, and decided to be quiet.

One of those mornings, Gandhi was sitting alone in front of his box. He had placed the metal shoe trees on the ground, waiting for some shoes. He saw Dr. John Davis coming in the distance. The American professor was walking, his dog next to him, a big dusty-colored German shepherd that growled and barked. Gandhi asked God for refuge from seeing him so early in the morning. Dr. Davis stopped in front of the shoe-shine box, holding the rope tied to the dog's neck, and the dog moved left and right, sniffing and putting his mouth on the shoe trees. The American pulled his dog back. And the dog would go close to the shoe trees and head in Gandhi's direction, sniff at the sitting man's feet, and Gandhi would try to get away from the dog, move his feet away, pretend to be busy with the shoe trees and shoes, and wipe his face with his long black sleeve. Dr. Davis asked how things were going, while the dog roamed about, with his master holding the rope. Then the dog got away from Davis's hand. The dog ran off, and Davis called him—"Fox! Fox!"—and the dog ran as if he'd found something. Dr. Davis left Gandhi and chased after his dog. A woman came and placed three pairs of men's black shoes in front of the box. Gandhi put them up on the shoe tree and started working. Gandhi didn't like to dye shoes until he'd stretched the leather out on the shoe tree. The original way of doing it, he believed, was to dye the shoes without taking them off the person's foot. The foot gave the shoe its form and stretched it out, and so the color would spread equally over the entire shoe. But when the shoe is without a foot, the leather gets wrinkled, and it becomes difficult to dye it, because the transformation to mirror becomes impossible.

Gandhi had finished mounting the shoes on the shoe trees when he saw Dr. Davis coming back with his dog. That day, John Davis made the suggestion that would make Gandhi leave his profession for the first time. He would leave it for the second and last time, based on a suggestion made by Hasan Zaylaa, when he would become responsible for keeping the quarter clean.

Mr. Davis stopped and asked him if he would help him feed his dog.

"I don't have anything, just shoes," Gandhi said.

Gandhi agreed to Mr. Davis's idea without ever imagining it would lead him to leave his trade.

Gandhi went into the American University cafeteria with a big burlap bag in his hand. Davis told him he'd made an arrangement with the kitchen manager and the American director of the kitchen to allow Gandhi to take the leftovers every day, take them to his house near Bakhaazi Hospital as food for Fox, who seemed he could never get enough to eat. He agreed with Gandhi to pay him one lira a day, and at that time a shoe shine was a quarter-lira. In other words, filling the bag was as good as shining four pairs of shoes.

When Gandhi entered the kitchen, he was shocked by the amount of food. The cook, who was wearing a white shirt and a long white cap on his head, led him through the inner rooms of the kitchen and pointed to the plates. Gandhi would empty everything from his bag. He'd fill the bag, and there would still be a lot of food left that was to be thrown away.

He took the bag to Mr. Davis's house, and that day he decided.

On the second day, he came with two bags—one for the dog and one for himself.

In the first bag he put the leftovers, and in the second one, which was stuffed with empty sardine tins he'd picked up the night before and had his wife wash out, he tried to sort out the food and place it in the little tin cans. Then he put them carefully into the bag.

On the third day, he brought, in addition to the two bags and the empty sardine tins, an empty bottle and tried to fill it with oil left in the plates of labneh.

On the fourth day, Fawziyya came with him, and she did the sorting and organizing of the food before it was placed into the tin cans.

On the fifth day, the routine was regulated, and he agreed with the kitchen manager to pay him six liras a day, after he'd refused Gandhi's offer to share the food.

On the sixth day, he opened a restaurant.

And on the seventh day, the day the American University cafeteria is closed, Gandhi rested in his house, and didn't go to work. That was the first time in his life he didn't go to work on a Sunday.

Gandhi placed some small chairs and handmade straw trays in front of his house in Nabaa and turned the stone bench into a restaurant.

"Those were the days," Gandhi would say. "In those days there was a lot of prosperity. We all ate, we and the dog. The dog had enough, and we had enough, and everyone ate ... " The Houranis started coming, Houranis, Kurds, all kinds of people, cement workers, port laborers, you name it, they'd come every day and buy. A plate of labneh, ten piasters, a plate of hummus, twenty-five, a plate of kefta, fifty, things just worked out. Muhammad al-Hariri, God rest his soul, started coming regularly. He'd come and bring a bottle of arak with him, and he'd pour some for himself and the other customers. I refused, I said no way, nothing sacrilegious in my restaurant, but how can you fight sacrilege when it's everywhere? So I drank, I had tons of money. Those were the days, I even forgot all about shoe shining—no, I didn't forget, I stopped sitting there all day, breaking my back behind the shoe-shine box. I worked a little on the side, for special customers. I'd take the box and sit beneath Madame Lillian Sabbagha's staircase, and enjoy seeing the beautiful Russian woman in the morning. I'd shine her shoes, the Reverend Amin's, Davis's, the Assyrian's, al-Munla's, and very few others. The real work, however, was in the restaurant."

Then came the catastrophe.

The dog died.

Gandhi was prepared for anyone's death, but not the dog's. Gandhi, like everyone, thought about death, and death, according to him, resembled his father, lying in the open coffin, teardrops stuck to his lower eyelids. He thought about his wife's death, and other people's deaths. Gandhi lived with death, the babies died before being born, death came before all things. Death was life. But the death of the dog never crossed his mind, and when the dog died, and Gandhi saw Mr. Davis transform into a ghost, he was beset with fear and worry. He tried to console the American, he tried to say to him what the Reverend Amin used to say when he'd visit him after all those still births that happened to Fawziyya, his wife. "The Lord giveth, and the Lord taketh away." He tried to console him but Mr. Davis went nuts. Davis would talk about how the murderer got out and spat, and he'd say he wanted to leave the country. His blond wife, who had some white strands in her hair like pieces of cloth planted on her scalp, sat with her head down in the corner of the house, curled up like a snail, hardly moving. Gandhi would go in and out, serve coffee to the few people who'd come to offer their condolences, and Davis would refuse to be consoled.

Gandhi's problem began two days later. He went to the cafeteria and was kicked out. The American head manager said "no more" and wouldn't let him in. The Arab manager who was peeking out the opening in the door said to him, "No more, there's no more food, the dog died, God rest his soul."

Gandhi tried to negotiate with him. He offered him double the six liras he was paying him every day, and half a bottle of oil every six months. The man refused. It seemed he wanted to take the leftovers himself, or he'd contracted them to someone else. Gandhi thought about asking Mr. Davis to talk to the head manager for him. But he was afraid of his grimace, he'd look at him with disgust and think he was despicable. The dog was dead and all this man could think about was his own disgusting financial gains. He tried to bring it up with Davis, but he backed off, worried about the possibility of those looks of disgust coming from the tall American.

The idea came from Madame Lillian.

He was sitting outside the entrance to his house, shining his customers' shoes, when he brought up the subject with her. He didn't tell her about the restaurant in Nabaa. He told her his future was ruined and that Davis had gone crazy after the death of his dog Fox.

She suggested he get another dog. At first Gandhi refused the idea completely, it gave him an eerie feeling, like some strange plant climbing up his feet, and he felt itchy all over. After two days of careful thought, and the Reverend Amin's advice, he changed his mind. He went to a store in Rawshi where they sold dogs, and paid a lot of money for "Little Fox." Little Fox looked exactly like the late Fox. Same color, same look, same movements, and same tongue. Gandhi picked him up and took him to his house in Nabaa. And there Fawziyya cried. "What a disgrace," she said, and cried.

Davis wouldn't take the little dog, and Suad nearly died with fear when she found him next to her in bed, and

Fawziyya would mop ten times a day trying to purge the house of this uncleanliness.

Gandhi picked up Little Fox and went to Davis's house. Davis wasn't home. His blond wife was there. When she saw the dog she started sobbing and crying. Gandhi, who was hugging the dog to his chest, tried to give him to her, but she refused to hold him. He went to hand the dog to her, but she didn't reach out for him. The dog fell to the floor and started barking in the middle of the house. Gandhi chased after him. He'd hid himself under the couch and was yelping. Gandhi laid down flat against the floor, on the orange carpet, and got him out. He picked him up again and went outside to wait for Mr. Davis.

When Davis came and saw the dog, he said no and started speaking in English. Gandhi didn't understand anything except the word *no,* and could see fear and confusion in the American professor's eyes. Gandhi picked up the dog and went home.

When Gandhi told Alice how he killed the dog, he was trying to change the subject from Nuha Aoun's murder, which had stirred up quite a commotion in the quarter. That day Malku the Assyrian decided to leave the country. He closed down his store for a week and told everyone he was going to sell it and go to Sweden, since the city was no longer ours. People were dying and the cats gnashed at them. Madame Aoun died, with all her hungry cats around her. There were three cats around the woman's dead body, and when the stench pervaded the area, people were shocked by the sight of the dust-covered cats with disheveled fur that looked as though they were wild.

Before she died, Madame Aoun had made up her mind and decided to marry Constantine Mikhbat. During their last telephone conversation, Constantine was in the hospital, having some routine tests, and asked her to come. She agreed, she said she'd come and marry him and live with him. Husn had known from the beginning that Madame Aoun would leave him to get married. He knew everything. That's what he told Rima, and Rima believed him. He said he didn't kill the woman, and she believed him. But no one believed him. Zaylaa would wink at him whenever he saw him and say, "Way to go, hotshot." Gandhi would avoid talking to him, and Master Ahmad became afraid of him.

Gandhi told Alice how the Reverend Amin gave him some Dimol and told him to mix it with milk, and how when he remembered the incident he thought about his daughter. "But I seek refuge from God, God forgive me." He took the Dimol and decided to finish with the whole story. The dog staggered. He drank it and started to stagger and fade, as if he wanted to sleep. The dog fell asleep, so Gandhi picked him up, wrapped him in newspapers, and threw him in front of the trash bin.

He told Alice he thought about the dog a lot the first few days of the war, when they were trapped in Nabaa and were choking from the smell of bombs falling everywhere. When they came to Hamra Street, things got better. It was no longer possible to go back to shining shoes. No one had his shoes shined anymore; we almost died of hunger and became destitute, until Zaylaa solved our problems.

Zaylaa said the quarter needed tidying up, and that was how it was. Gandhi became the general overseer of cleanliness for the people's committee.

Spiro with the hat came to only one of the committee meetings and then stopped coming. He told Zaylaa he was with them heart and soul, but he didn't like to be active in politics.

Spiro was surprised at the first committee meeting. He didn't see any of the respected residents of the quarter there. Abu Saeed al-Munla was absent, Muhammad Ainati didn't come, and the Maqdisi boys had disappeared. All that remained was a group of people who'd been kicked out of their homes from other parts of the country, Zaylaa, Gandhi the shoe shiner, and women from the Montana nightclub.

"What kind of a shitty committee is this?" Spiro said to the Assyrian.

But Habib Malku didn't go along with him on this, for Malku knew from past experience that you have to bow your head in wartime. That's what he said to Father John, trying to persuade him to come to the committee meetings.

"If you come, Father, I will. We all will."

The priest preferred to stay neutral. "We are staying neutral, with them and not with them. Tomorrow things will topple, my son, it's better they don't topple on us. Right now, leave them alone, leftists and Palestinians and I don't know what, okay, but tomorrow it'll topple. Now we're with them, and when things topple, we'll remain with them, the important thing is that things don't fall on top of us."

Everything toppled.

Alice said she came to the quarter, and everything had turned upside down. She came by chance after the Blow Up shut down and she found herself out of work. Her furnished room in Ayn Mraysi became a burden to her, and the war started, and the young women started emigrating from Beirut. The emigration began on "Black Saturday." On that day in December 1975, everything got mixed up. Armed men attacked the people, and there was a lot of death. The Phalangists, with their masks, were in the city, murdering people and tossing the corpses all over the place. From that day on, the masks became commonplace.

Everyone wore masks and Beirut died that day, couldn't walk anymore, armed men came out like madmen, and bullets whizzed over the heads of the innocent. That day the war turned against the people, and the bodies strewn in the streets swelled before anyone had a chance to take them to the cemetery.

Alice said that after that the emigration of the young women began. Ayn Mraysi area shuddered that frightful night, and the bombs rained down on Zaytooni, where the bars that had been abandoned by their owners were. Everyone started to think about leaving. Alice didn't leave, she thought about going back to Shekka. She was sitting in her room, alone, thinking about going back to a house she remembered nothing about. But she didn't go back. Yes, she went back once, and everything was gone. She went back to see her father, but she didn't see him. They told her about him. They told her at the end he'd become the size of a baby and cried all the time, and that the woman who was living with him would sit beside him and cry. He died before she had a chance to see him. She had no memory of him. She didn't even see his face that night. Alice was a child and darkness filled the place. She didn't see his face.

"I forgave him," Alice said. "God forgive me for forgiving him. He died and I didn't see him, he lived and he didn't see me, you never know, even when you know, you don't know. When he came, he left, and when I wanted him it was all over. Things end where they should begin. It's all a big lie, this whole life is like one big lie."

Alice completed the lie. She said she accepted a job at the Montana because there was no other way. She'd become like a beggar. Once Zaylaa told her she was a beggar, he told her the worst thing about women was that they all wind up beggars in the end, and he thanked God he was a man. Alice told him she wasn't exactly sure he was a man.

A man doesn't do that. That day he'd hit her, in the bar in front of everyone, and that day Alice cried in front of everyone and decided never to go back to work. But she went back.

"Being a waitress in a bar is better than being dead," she said to Gandhi.

And Gandhi would agree with her, and tell her life was difficult, that Suad had driven him to the brink of madness, and that he was worried about her.

When Vitsky was found dead in her small apartment, no one dared to go in except Alice. They were all afraid. That day, Alice took Madame Lillian and led her inside, and Lillian began to scream like a madwoman, and dragged the Reverend Amin, who'd already begun his journey to the next world after his wife abandoned him, through the coals.

Alice sat alone in the Salonica Hotel, unable to find herself a real job. Even cleaning rooms became impossible. She found it difficult to hold a broom because of her trembling hands, and the owner of the hotel would look at her with false sympathy.

Abd al-Hakim the Egyptian was nostalgic for the old days in this country, for this hotel used to be the meeting place of the upper crust of society. It was an oasis, almost like an oasis. Kuwaitis and other Gulf Arabs would come and stay one night there, and Abd al-Hakim was the owner of the one-nighter. Now, what was happening? The hotel had gone to ruins, and he couldn't leave it. If he left it he'd lose the fortune he'd put into building it, stone by stone. He'd stay, as he would say, because the war would end and things would go back to the way they were.

Alice would say that things would never go back to the way they were. She lived in the hotel with retired prostitutes—four Egyptian and one Syrian—and three women from Beirut looking for work and not finding anything but sleeping with soldiers and armed men who paid very little if anything at all, and the hotel was transformed into something like a nursing home.

Alice said the hotel those days had become a lot like the nursing home she took the Reverend Amin to. There she saw the nun who looked like this man, and she'd point to Abd al-Hakim the Egyptian, and men collapsed onto wheelchairs, and she smelled shit everywhere. And here, too, the smell of shit wouldn't go away.

"I mop everything with soap, but when you live in shit, how can you expect the smell to go away?"

I asked Alice about Husn, and his connection to Madame Nuha's murder. She said she didn't know. She said, "Husn isn't sure he killed her. It's true for a while he acted like he was a warrior, but he didn't fight. Husn didn't go to war. He carried a gun like everyone, but he didn't fight. I don't know anyone who did. None of them fought. What kind of war is this where no one is fighting, but it still goes on? The war continues with no goal. Husn didn't fight, he carried a gun, and the shithead, excuse my language, became a big man and started believing he could act like one. But he was in love with the beauty salon. He carried the gun against his father's will. But what did he do? Nothing. He said he went and fought for a few days in the business district, I saw him carrying stolen goods, him and Zaylaa. They went and robbed the place, no one actually fought. All those who fought died, and all those who didn't fight died, death and more death, my son, what is this mess?"

For two years Alice had been living in the Salonica Hotel. The Montana opened its doors after the Israeli withdrawal from Beirut, which led to the massacres of Sabra and Shatila, but Alice didn't go back to the Montana. One of the Egyptian girls told her Zaylaa was asking about her. Alice said, "Forget it, I've retired, I'm going to stay in this hotel, and I'll die in this hotel." And she stayed in the hotel. When I went there to ask about her after the war broke out again in 1984, I didn't find anyone. The hotel was in ruins, some armed men surrounded it. I didn't ask the men about Alice, or Abd al-Hakim the Egyptian. I went home and decided to go and ask Zaylaa.

At the Montana, I didn't find Zaylaa. I found a man that resembled him. Alice had described him to me. She said he was dark-skinned, had a broken front tooth, a thick neck, and a low, husky voice that seemed to come from deep down in his belly. At the entrance of the Montana I saw a man with this description, so I asked him about Zaylaa.

"Which Zaylaa?"

"Hasan Zaylaa, the tough guy, the one in charge of the Montana, isn't that who you are?" I answered him.

"There's no Zaylaa."

"Please. I'm looking for a woman called Alice."

"Alice what?"

"I don't know. Alice, that woman who's around sixty years old who used to work here selling flowers."

"What flowers? We don't sell flowers."

"O.K. Husn, do you know Husn?"

"What are you, the police? Running an interrogation? This is a bar called the Montana, there's no Alice, no Husn, no.flowers, there are whores, if you want one, we can arrange it, and we'll give you a good price, too."

Alice was lost, they were all lost.

Even Rima. I didn't find a trace of her. They said they saw her once. She came to Spiro with the hat's house to ask about Husn. He said he didn't know.

Spiro was bedridden, in pain. They said he had lung cancer. He was always asking to see Little Spiro, whose name wasn't Spiro. He moaned in bed, holding an icon of the Virgin Mary, and shouted "O, mother of light," and mother of light didn't answer.

Rima came once to visit him and ask about Ralph, but Ralph wasn't there. Spiro didn't know who this Ralph was, and when she called him by his other name, he shook his head and told her Madame Aoun had suffered a lot before she died. He said he saw her in a dream. She was standing under a shower with blood coming out of it instead of water. He started crying.

Rima left and didn't go back. After that, no one in the quarter saw her again.

As for Habib Malku, he left the country. He disappeared from the quarter, then people saw the store open again, a new owner inside, and new goods. Malku sold everything and went to Sweden.

No one remained.

Little Gandhi's house was returned to the property owner after he paid Zaylaa twenty thousand liras. Zaylaa took the money, sold Little Gandhi's things, and gave the house back to the owner, who rented it out as a warehouse for pharmaceutical supplies.

Beirut was different that morning. Morning carried the smell of death. There were armed men everywhere, and commotion, as if those who had died never died, as if the war hadn't ended, as if it had just begun.

6

Alice said he died.

"I came and saw him, I covered him with newspapers, there was no one around, his wife disappeared, they all disappeared, and I was all alone."

Alice said she took him to the cemetery, and she saw the people without faces. "People have become faceless," she told me. She spoke to them and didn't get any response, then she left them and went on her way. That's how the story ended.

"Tell me about him," I said to her.

"How shall I tell you?" she answered. "I was living as though I were living with him without realizing it. When you live, you don't notice things. I didn't notice, I just don't know." She shook her head and repeated her sentence. "All I know is, he died, and he died for nothing."

I recall Alice's words and try to imagine what happened, but I keep finding holes in the story. All stories are full of holes. We no longer know how to tell stories, we don't know anything anymore. The story of Little Gandhi ended. The journey ended, and life ended.

That's how the story of Abd al-Karim Husn al-Ah-

madi al-Mughayiri, otherwise known as Little Gandhi, ended.

During my last encounter with Alice she said she was going to leave the country. She was sad, and looked at things differently, as if she weren't really seeing things, or as if things had slipped out of her hands, and out of her memory. She'd been drinking arak a lot, and quarreling with Abd al-Hakim and his hotel guests. She'd go out a lot to walk along the seacoast, near Haj Dawwod Café, which had become a heap of rubble. She'd come back in the evening and wouldn't clean the rooms. She wouldn't do anything. Abd al-Hakim the Egyptian asked her to help him find some girls, and she laughed.

"Forget it, son, the girls are all with the soldiers, what do you take me for, the government?"

Alice wasn't the government. She walked alone, without leaning on anything. She hardly slept. She'd get up at five in the morning, go out on the corniche, and walk. When she'd get tired, she'd sit on a rock, alone, and her eyes would travel far away.

What did she think about? Was she reliving the old days? Did she see herself with the eyes of her soul? Or did memory take her to eyes that didn't see her, bringing back the fire of those long-gone days, and so ending with them the last drops of life?

Alice wasn't thinking about anything, for she was lying. I told her she was lying. No, I didn't tell her. When she said to me, "I'm full of lies," it crossed my mind that she was lying to me, and I was sure she was lying when I found out everyone knew the story of "The Leader," and they attributed it to more than one woman.

Alice knew, for when she took the Reverend Amin to the nursing home, she discovered things were fading away, as if they'd never been. When she got back she asked Little

Gandhi about the Reverend Amin as a young man. Gandhi didn't know how to answer. He responded with short phrases, as if he didn't remember.

Did Amin exist, or not? Did she? What was the difference?

I asked her if she remembered any details. I asked about the stories, and I discovered she didn't remember anything, as though she didn't want to remember.

She said to me, "That ass Abd al-Hakim doesn't know who I am. Yes, he does know, but he doesn't know. Man is ephemeral." She said man is ephemeral.

Ever since she saw Gandhi's final hour, and the image of his wife and daughter leaving in the middle of that rain that scorched Beirut the morning of September 15, 1982, she changed. She saw things only at the moment they happened. By herself, she took him to the cemetery, as if he were a relative. There was no one with her. By herself she got the sheikh and the coffin and the shroud. She told the people at the Islamic Nursing Home to perform the ablution. They said no, they don't wash martyrs, they are cleansed by their own blood. "But he is poor, he had nothing to do with it." They said he was a martyr. She took him and buried him without the ablution, he was washed by the rain and the mud and the shots. As if he never was. Even his face was erased from her memory, all their faces were erased. She remembered nothing of them but small flashes that came and faded in her memory.

Alice didn't go back to the Montana. She found out her feet couldn't anymore, and that night was no longer night, it had been disclosed, like a broken watermelon. And days became filled with straw. What really bothered her was that the taste in her mouth had started to change. Before the taste in her mouth changed, she didn't know the mouth was so important, and that when the tongue becomes stiff and thick in the mouth, it becomes a burden on the person. Her tongue was dry, and she was frightened by the taste in her mouth that gave her the feeling death was near.

Once she told me about her death. She said things I don't remember, and I can't compose. She said how death was the end of comfort, death was the beginning of weariness. I didn't understand what she meant until I went to search for her at the nursing home in Ashrafiyyeh. I went and asked about the Reverend Amin, and so the nun came out to see me. I left without finding out anything. Everything had changed. After ten years of war Ashrafiyyeh had changed. "Little Mountain" was no longer a mountain, it had become like back roads we don't know well. People's faces changed. Even the old smell, I didn't find, except in Saint Mitr Cemetery.

I asked the nun and she said she hadn't heard the name Reverend Amin before, and that they didn't take in anyone from other denominations. I told her Alice brought him in 1981, and I tried to describe this man, whom I'd never seen in my life. The nun said she knew nothing about it, and she'd been there for twenty years. She'd never seen a Protestant minister in her life. I said the man was senile, maybe he'd forgotten his name, maybe he was there under a different name, and I tried to remember the Greek words Alice told me he'd use to pray all day long.

I asked her about Alice, had she come to the nursing home.

She asked me her family name.

I said, I don't know.

She asked me about her relatives.

I said, I don't know.

She asked me who she was.

I said, I don't know.

The nun said I was asking about imaginary names, she didn't know any Alice, or any Reverend, and she doubted my mental competence.

I asked her where they buried the people who died at the nursing home. She said they didn't bury them, their relatives would come and take care of all that.

And those who had no relatives? I asked.

Those we bury in the nursing home cemetery, then they're taken a year or more later, depending on the decay of the corpse, and placed in a well.

I asked her if they wrote the names of the deceased on the nursing home graves.

She said no. She asked me why I was asking such questions, so I smiled. The nun said I was crazy, and that I was asking about things that didn't exist. She patted me on the shoulder and told me the war had made everyone lose their minds. She offered me a cup of coffee. I drank it quickly and burnt my tongue, and I left the nursing home.

I went to Saint Mitr Cemetery. I searched among the scattered graves beneath the cypress trees. I read all the names, and on a half-destroyed grave, whose white tile had become dust-colored, I saw the image of Alice. I went closer and read the name, it was someone else, but the image engraved on the semiwhite marble resembled Alice as a young woman. That's how I imagined Alice in her youth, with a full face, thick lips, a small turned-up nose, big eyes. I went closer to Alice, or to whom I thought was Alice, and I read my own name, and I read my mother's name, and I read my grandfather's name. They were all there, there wasn't a face I saw that I hadn't seen before, it was like a long dream from which I couldn't wake up.

I stood there a long time, then I came back to where I was, behind this green table, beneath this orange light in which the light fades. I closed my eyes and saw Gandhi. I saw a short man walking between the walls of the city. The city was made up of opposing walls, and the short man was walking, the shoe-shine box hanging around his neck, his head banging against the walls as he tried to find his way. He walked between the walls, stretching his hands out as if he were swimming in water that circled around him, swallowing him down.

The water that is swallowing him sweeps me away to the abyss, where I walk, and see all their faces: Spiro and Fawziyya and Malku and Suad and Abd al-Hakim and Davis, and Nuha and Lillian and Constantine and Abu Abbas and Tannous, and Abu Jamil and Husn and Rima and Sheikh Zakariyya and the Gypsy woman and the dog and Doctor Atef and Father John and Alice and Sunbuk and Abu Hurayra's tomb, and Zaylaa and "The Leader" and Alfred and Vitsky and Simaan Fayyad and his grandfather and Bishop Athanasios and the nun and Joséf and Master Ahmad and the little mountain and Shukri the poet, and Saint Spirodonious and his donkeys, and the soldiers' black boots, and the newspapers whose words fled from them, and the vendors, and Abu Saeed al-Munla sleeping under the screams of his minaret, and Malku, who immigrated to Sweden, and Little Spiro, whose name was Nabil.

I see them and I see the faces of the soldiers, from where did the city get filled up with soldiers? The city is dimming, its trees are burning, and the soldiers start the fires.

I told Alice, but she wasn't with me. She promised me she'd come with me. She promised me she'd take me to visit them all. But she didn't come. When I decided to meet them, she disappeared, and when I went to look for her, I didn't find the grave. She left me without letting me know anything. She took all the knowledge and left.

When I tell it, I don't tell anything. I tell about it and I don't quench my thirst, and I go on my journey to it, and don't find it. I find words that dangle like a rope, I climb the rope and I slip, and when I tumble to the ground, I see the walls collapse and the city migrate.

Alice didn't fool me. She lied to me a lot. She knew I wanted to hear stories for the sake of hearing stories. She let me hear what I wanted, and when I wanted to stop hearing the stories, I discovered that the stories died beneath my pen.

7

That's how the story ended.

Little Gandhi was, a man who lived and died, like millions of men, on the face of this spinning earth.

He was born in Mashta Hasan, ran away from his father, who took him to his grandfather's cave, worked in the "key's" Bakery in Tripoli, moved to Beirut, where he worked at Abu Ayoun's restaurant, and then worked as a shoe shiner. He got married and had two children, Husn and Suad. Husn was a barber, and Suad was sick. He loved life and loved the flavor of it. Alice told him, and the Reverend Amin befriended him, and Davis turned him into a restaurant owner, and the dog died, and Gandhi grieved over the dog more than he grieved over his own father.

Gandhi died.

He died when Beirut fell beneath the black shoes. He didn't know that he died. He sensed death before it came, then when he died, he didn't know. And so the bullets didn't hurt him, and death came lightly, like a short dream that doesn't end.

Gandhi died, and Alice became a maid at the Salonica Hotel. The Reverend Amin became senile and ended up in a nursing home. The American went back to his country, and Malku immigrated to Sweden, and Spiro died trying to give his name to his grandson.

A long journey, because it's short.

Journeys always last long because they fall short. The man in whose eyes the world clouded up tried to take on life with his kabbout. The doctor laughed at the kabbout, and the pharmacist acted like a clown, and Gandhi died.

His name was not Gandhi.

Abd al-Karim, son of Husn, son of Abd al-Karim, son of Husn, son of Abd al-Karim, son of Husn, and all the way back to Noah.

They named him Gandhi and he didn't know why.

But he knew why he died, he knew the bullets weren't aimed at him, but rather at the heart of a city that destroyed itself, because it was like Gandhi, it was trying to make a story out of its name.

And the story is a game of names. "And he taught Adam all the names." When we knew the names, the story began, and when the names were extinguished, the story began.

Elias Khoury is the editor of the literary supplement of *al-Nahar* newspaper in Beirut. He has taught at the American University of Beirut and at Columbia University in New York. Khoury has published book-length works in various genres, including novels, critical essays, and short stories. He is the author of the novels *Little Mountain,* which was published in English by the University of Minnesota Press in 1989, and *The Journey of Little Gandhi,* which was published in Beirut in 1989. The University of Minnesota Press also published his *Gates of the City* in 1993.

Sabah Ghandour teaches in the Department of Asian and Middle Eastern Studies at the University of Pennsylvania.

Paula Haydar is a freelance translator living in Fayetteville, Arkansas.